SHALLOWS

SHALLOWS

denver evans

*For my man, who is all the best parts of Emerson.
Thank you for loving this story.*

CAYAN ISLANDS

CONTENTS

SONG

He couldn't breathe.
Water alternately pushed and pulled at him.
Suspended.
Straining.
His lungs burned and he wanted his mother.
A song. Music. Words.
Mother?
No, but a sea shanty she often sang over him.
Music in the water. Words.
Something pushing harder than the waves.
Sand.
Air.
Breath.
Mother.

Emerson woke up in a cold sweat, his clenched fists shaking and causing the muscles in his arms to cramp. He drew a gasping breath that sent his head spinning. He was in his own bed, the one he was nearly too long for. No water enveloped him, he wasn't drowning.

He sat up and scrubbed his eyes, trying to regulate his too-quick breathing. It had just been a dream.

The dream. It had been *the* dream. The one that had plagued him for years and had given him an unnaturally strong fear of the sea. The one that had returned more frequently and vividly each year around the Hunting Time ever since he could remember.

17 years is too long to have the same nightmare.

He grimaced in the barely grey light. It was just before dawn, he reckoned. With a sudden, restless movement, he threw off his quilt and stood. Quietly, he slipped into his trousers and loose white shirt. He carried his boots with him, walking softly on stocking feet as to not waken his mother. At the door of their cottage, he slipped the scuffed black boots on and laced them quickly. Snatching his heavy woolen coat from its peg, he donned it and then pulled a newsboy cap down over unruly black hair.

With stealth that came of far too much practice, he opened the door at just the right speed to avoid the creaking it was prone to. Slipping out into the predawn chill, he let his feet carry him to a worn path just beyond the small cottage.

The path began smooth and sandy, but quickly became rocky and steep. After several minutes, Emerson reached the top and turned toward the sea. A stiff breeze blew in, as was always the case this close to the shore. It pushed at his unbuttoned wool coat, rippling the thinner fabric of his shirt.

He didn't feel the cold, for his ears were straining to hear through the noise of the breeze moaning around the cliff and the waves breaking down below.

He reached the edge of the cliff and stood a moment, letting the wind drive him back a foot or two. His mother would worry if she could see him.

Dropping to one knee, he closed his eyes and listened with all he was worth.

Nothing.

Without realizing it, he held his breath as if the very sound of his own breathing might be drowning out the song he listened for. After a moment, a familiar feeling of panic crawled up his throat, and he took a gasping breath, falling back to a sitting position.

Emerson cursed quietly under his breath, amazed at his own weakness. He snatched the cap off his head and ran frustrated fingers through the tangle of his hair.

He turned the cap around in his hands, staring at it unseeingly. The cold finally penetrated his thoughts, and he closed up his coat, replacing his cap on his head. *I'm such a fool. Why do I keep doing this? Why does the sea terrify me and yet call to me with the faint memory of a song?*

He shook his head, as if trying to clear it. *Who expects the sea to yield a song? Am I mad?*

But the fact remained: something told him the sea had sung to him once. It was like his dream, but more vivid. More like a memory.

"But how is that possible?" he shouted at the dark waves before him.

The sea didn't answer, but a voice inside Emerson spoke up. *People really will think you're crazy if you keep on trying to hold conversations with the waves. Imagine how your mother would feel if she'd seen that.*

Wondering why his inner voice had such a way with words when his mouth didn't, Emerson stood and stuffed his hands in the warm, wooly pockets of his coat. He was about to turn and take the path back down the cliff when something caught his eye.

In the distance, a faint blueish glow illuminated the dark water. It was joined by another and then another.

"The mermaids are about," he whispered to himself. He shuddered, not bothering to tell himself it was just the wind. Even the burly, brave fishermen at the docks would shudder at the sight of that many mermaids in their waters. They spoke in hushed tones and with drawn faces, telling stories of encounters with the semi-transparent, luminescent creatures.

They never broke the surface of the water, but instead floated just below it, staring sailors right in the eyes and mouthing words no one could hear.

They could only be seen well when it was dark or nearly so, but according to the sailors, that meant they might be around but not easily visible during the day.

Children were taught from their first toddling moments to never go near the shore.

Especially during the Hunting Time.

Once a year, mermaids would swim in close to the island of Azul and the others in the chain. Fishing boats would remain docked for days and only venture out when the last of the glowing creatures had gone further out into the depths.

Emerson blinked.

From his vantage point on the cliff, he could just make out the Chadwick beach and his mother's cottage. The village was a shadow beyond, set back a safe distance from the water. Fishing boats bobbed somewhere in the darkness.

None of this drew his attention, however, a single mermaid glowed faintly—much closer to the shore than the rest. He swallowed hard as her light made a turn, seemingly toward the cottage. She swam parallel to the shoreline for a bit, and then made her way closer to the cliff where he stood.

He moved closer to the edge and looked down. The faint glow had stopped just beneath him, the mermaid's actual form impossible to distinguish through the waves rushing to meet the cliff. He waited a moment, hoping against hope that it was coincidence she'd stopped just below him.

She didn't move.

The Hunting.

Emerson took a few steps back from the edge.

"Emerson!"

He started violently and jumped backward—further from the edge—landing on his rear.

"Emerson! What are you doing?"

He grimaced, recognizing the voice.

"Saria," he said, trying to keep the exasperation out of his voice. How did she manage to make everything sound like a taunt?

"Why do you care?" he asked, picking himself up.

There was no reply for a moment, and he turned to find her hunched into her brown coat. The wind whipped the hem of her russet red skirt around the ankles of her boots, and tossed her curls in a caramel-colored frenzy. The tip of her nose was red and she looked a little winded.

"You really think I came up that steep path just to annoy you, Emerson?" she asked.

Why don't you just add "stupid" to the end of that? He thought, but didn't say anything.

She shook her head before staring out at the sea for a moment. Finally she spoke. "I didn't think you wanted the whole village to see you up here standing on the edge of a cliff at dawn. I figured you might not realize how light it was getting and that someone could probably see you." She bit her lip. "I'm sorry I bothered you."

Before he could process exactly what she'd said—much less respond, she was hurrying back down the path in a flurry of russet skirts.

He glanced around him, realizing she was right. It was light enough now, that everyone in the village would be able to see the crazy son of poor Idina Kadwell standing on the cliff, as if ready to fall to his death.

Emerson glanced back at the sea. It looked grey in the early morning light, and no glowing mermaids punctuated the waves.

He turned and headed back to the path, his thoughts turning to the project waiting in his workshop.

But why had the sea not sung to him?

VILLAGE

Emerson flipped through his tattered, leather-bound notebook. Where was that sketch of an alternative way to rig his pulley system? He frowned and rubbed his forehead. The quietness of the workshop enveloped him peacefully. Thinking was usually so smooth and easy in silence like this. His mother wasn't even clattering around the kitchen on the other side of the workshop wall. She had gone outside to hang the washing on the line.

Slowly turning in a circle, he searched the small room for his other notebook. There. On top of a keg of pitch. He opened it and quickly located the sketch. He compared what he'd been tinkering with to the two drawings and thought for a moment.

"The distance between the bracket in here and the bracket in the kitchen..." he glanced up at the hand-sized hole he'd cut in the wall between the two rooms. "I'm going to need more rope."

Snatching up a small pouch of coins and his cap, he ran out of the workshop and into the kitchen, banging the door shut behind him.

He met his mother coming inside with an empty clothes basket. Her slightly-greying hair was windswept from the sea breeze, curls dancing out of the knot she kept it in. The corners of her eyes crinkled, and she smiled at the sight of him.

"I'm finished with the washing now, son," she began. "Oh—! Where are you off to in such a hurry? Will you be back for dinner?"

"Yes, Mum," Emerson said, nodding. "I'll be back in time. I don't have enough rope for the message pulley. I've thought up a new way to rig it, and—well anyway, I'm getting some more rope from the market."

"We have rope in the lean-to if you'd like to use it," his mother said, gesturing vaguely outside.

"I need thinner rope. That stuff is good for use on a fishing boat, but not for my pulley."

"Oh, I see. Any requests for dinner?"

"Naw, anything you make will be great." He looked thoughtful for a moment. "Although a boiled egg would be nice. And maybe some of that ham we had yesterday. And—well now I'm getting hungry. I'd better hurry." Emerson leaned down and kissed his mother's cheek before jogging away from the cottage.

He could feel her watching him, so he turned and waved. She smiled and waved back before shutting the door.

There was likely to be a boiled egg and some ham ready by the time he got home again. *I have a good mother.*

Emerson had mixed feelings about trips to the village market. Though small, it was too noisy and full of people to allow for very good thinking. But—oh— the things he could buy there! Things to eat, things to tinker with, gifts he knew would delight his mother. It was hard to keep from spending all his coin. But when one was not a fisherman in a fishing village, coin could be hard to come by.

Rope, he told himself. *Rope, and nothing else. In and out; no fuss.*

He made his way to a booth he knew would have an assortment of rope thicknesses and types. When the portly merchant finished with another customer, he turned toward Emerson with an eyebrow raised.

"I'm looking for some rope," Emerson began. "I'd like something thinner than what they use on the docks—maybe as big around as my finger?"

The merchant shrugged, his bulk causing his neck to all but disappear. "Sure I have that. But if yer looking for rope to hang yourself, I don't see why you'd be picky about the size!" He guffawed loudly.

Emerson knit his eyebrows, confused. "Hang myself—?"

"Well, you're the crazy lad who was standing all toe-to-toe with the cliff this morning, ain't ya? Decided jumping wasn't your—"

Emerson felt his face burning. "I'll see if someone else has what I need," he said quietly and stiffly. People at neighboring booths were staring.

"Kid has always had a death wish," he heard someone murmur.

He forced himself not to bolt from the market; it would only draw more attention to him. And currently that was the last thing he wanted. If only the ground would swallow him up!

Once he safely made it away from the busyness, he paused in a side street and took a steadying breath. He turned his hands over, realizing they were shaking.

Stupid reaction.

Here he was in a side street shaking from embarrassment. And anger at having been embarrassed in front of what must have been the entire village of Chadwick. At being singled out of the crowd as the butt of a ghastly joke.

His feet beat a rhythm on the path back to the cottage.

Always different.

Bookworm.

Not a fisherman.

Nothing like Father.

Lazy tinkerer.

Not tough, not tanned.

Quiet not bold.

And crazy.

SHALLOWS

It's a good thing they don't know the truth. Better they think I have a death wish than to know I wake up at night thinking the sea will sing to me.

RUMORS

His mother glanced over her shoulder in surprise when he opened the door.

"That didn't take you long," she commented. "Did they have what you needed?" She registered his expression and straightened, turning to face him. "What is it?"

"It's nothing," he mumbled. He never wanted to worry her, but either his face wouldn't comply or she was far too perceptive.

"Emerson. What's going on?"

"Someone teased me," he said. "You know I have a hard time taking teasing. I'll be fine, though." He had hoped he could just pass it off to her as no big deal and then never have to think of it again. But as soon as the words left his mouth, he realized if the village was aware of his early morning hike, his mother would soon be as well. Better to tell her the truth than have her worried by a rumor.

"Early this morning I had my nightmare again, so I hiked the cliff for a little fresh air. Someone must have seen me up there as the sun was rising. One of the merchants joked I had been thinking of jumping. It was embarrassing."

A little pucker appeared between his mother's eyebrows.

So much for not worrying her! Emerson scrambled to make it disappear. "It's a silly thing for him to say, don't you think? I mean, with the beauty of a sunrise over the water who would want to jump off anything? I certainly didn't." Emerson watched his words smooth away the concern on his mother's face.

"I'm sorry, Emrie. People will talk about anything, whether true or false. Just because they find it an amusing rumor to spread of an afternoon doesn't make it true, though. There's comfort in that at least."

Emerson nodded. His mother was right, but it still made him feel queasy.

She patted his back and then gave him a little push in the direction of the table. "Let's eat a bite of dinner."

He almost protested until he saw the exact food he'd mentioned waiting on his plate. *Ah, mum. You're so good to me.*

After helping his mother with the washing up, Emerson burrowed back into his workshop. Throughout the meal, his mind had been turning over a way to rig the pulley without the extra length of rope. He had visualized a possible design and had tried to hold onto the picture in his mind's eye until the last dish was dried.

Now his pencil moved feverishly over the notebook page, barely keeping up with his thoughts. He sketched and jotted notes about the pieces he'd drawn. The pencil's scratching was the only sound he heard, not processing the light knock on the cottage door nor his mother's voice greeting a visitor.

Only when Saria spoke behind him, did he realize she had arrived. He jumped and nearly destroyed a nearby model of another invention with his elbow.

"Saria! Hang it all!" he scowled, inspecting the piece he had broken off the model. Setting it down, he shifted his feet and glanced up at her with a quick, "Sorry."

His mother had taught him to use better language than that. Especially in front of ladies. Not that Saria—with all her taunting and the way she looked down on him—was particularly a *lady*.

His eyes wandered back to the notebook page. What had he been about to write when she spoke?

"I heard what happened in the market," she said, her voice lilting annoyingly.

"Of course you did," Emerson sighed. *Why* did she insist on tormenting him?

"They only tease you because you're different, you know. They're saying you were going to jump off the cliff, but I—"

He rounded on her with a disgusted look. "It was you, wasn't it! Don't think you can act concerned for my reputation, then be the one to spread rumors, and think I won't realize it was you who did it!"

Her eyes widened theatrically, and he turned away from her again. He didn't want to watch her drama. "I may not be a tough sailor like everyone else around here," he growled in a low voice, "but I sure as blazes am not an idiot."

Well, apparently I get eloquent when I'm upset.

He clamped his mouth shut. He'd already shown her too much of how affected he was. That was probably exactly what she'd been hoping for: a reaction. Spreading rumors and then coming to rub his face in the fact that he was different!—why had his mother even let her in?

Behind him, Saria didn't say anything. Then, in a rush of skirts she was gone.

Emerson was glad. It seemed like she was always on hand at his worst moments.

Now what *had* he been about to write? He had absolutely no idea. *That girl!*

"Emerson Bailey Kadwell!" His mother's voice filled the small cottage. He jumped. His mother never sounded like that.

He came to the doorway of the workshop. "Yes, Mum?" he said, regarding her warily.

She frowned at him with more displeasure than he thought he'd ever seen on her face. "What, *exactly*, did you say to Miss Beggley to make her leave our home in tears?"

SECRETS

"What did you say to Saria?" Emerson's mother asked again.

Emerson sighed. "Look, Mum—she's the one who told everybody about me being on the cliff. Saria started the rumor. And then she had the nerve to come here and rub it in my face and basically tell me if I just weren't so different, nobody would've teased me."

His mother closed her eyes and sighed. "And what did *you* say, Emerson?"

"Just that I didn't appreciate her acting concerned and then spreading rumors. And that while I might be less than the ideal young man in this village, I'm not a complete idiot." Emerson folded his arms.

He realized he probably looked defiant rather than self-protective. He didn't like being at odds with his mother, so he dropped his arms by his sides and waited.

After a moment, his mother sighed. "Emrie, I understand the feeling of frustration, I really do. People in this village have regarded you less than favorably."

27

Emerson could feel the "but" coming.

"But, son, you always have a choice about how to respond. Now, perhaps your point was a good one, if that's indeed what she did. But can't you think of any other way to have said it?"

Emerson studied the floor. Of course now that the whole thing was over, his mind flooded with other options. "Mum, does she really deserve having her feelings coddled after what she did?"

"After what you *think* she did. Being kind is never coddling someone. And, Emrie? This isn't about whether she deserved something or not. It's about you being the best person you can be regardless of whether anyone else is. That's all you can control after all."

Emerson gave his mother a half-smile and sighed. "You know how much I hate it that you make so much sense all the time."

She squeezed his shoulder and moved to begin working on supper. "Just think about it?"

He gave a nod.

"Oh, and Emrie? Mr. Hammer asked me if you'd be helping the men with the fencing of the shore again this year. There have been enough sightings already they plan to start tomorrow morning."

"I'll be there."

She laid out some potatoes and an onion. Emerson wiped the potatoes clean and set to chopping them with the large kitchen knife. His mother peeled the onion and then chopped it too when Emerson had finished with the knife. They worked in companionable silence punctuated by sniffles once the onion was cut.

Usually he teased her about feeling so sorry for cutting up a vegetable, but today his mind was elsewhere. He watched as she transferred the potato and onion pieces to a pot before filling it with fresh water from the jug in the corner. She set it to boil on the stove.

"Mum?"

"Yes?"

"When I was at the market—" he broke off and paused for a moment. Did he really want to ask the question that had just popped into his head? It seemed unlikely, but what if there was something to it? "Well," he continued, "one of the villagers muttered something that sounded like, 'that kid has always had a death wish.'"

He watched his mother closely. She merely stared at the spoon she was holding, rubbing something invisible off the handle.

"What did he mean?" Emerson asked. "Did something happen when I was little?"

His mother frowned ever so slightly. "I never asked: does soup sound good to you?" She gestured toward the nearly-boiling pot.

Emerson blinked at the sudden change of subject. "Um—yes—sure. But did something happen or... almost happen to me when I was little?"

She didn't answer.

Emerson felt a familiar panic crawling up from his chest.

"Mum—it's the nightmare, isn't it?"

She looked at him briefly, her eyes showing regret and something else. Maybe fear? "You can work on your pulley. I'll call you when supper is ready."

Words stuck in Emerson's throat, so he turned and walked into his workshop. Closing the door quietly behind him, he leaned against it while trying to slow his breathing. His hands were clenched. They'd begin shaking soon if he didn't get his breathing under control.

He crossed to the workbench and picked up one of his models, turning it around in the fading light coming through the window. He searched every inch of it for an area that he might be able to redesign and improve. After a few moments, his breathing slowed.

Setting the model down gently, he leaned both hands against the workbench.

She hadn't answered him.

It had to be the nightmare. Had he really almost drowned in the sea at some point in his life? When? Why couldn't he remember it?

He could tell the question and its answer disturbed his mother. She had been working so hard to keep her emotions in check. He ran a hand through his hair in exasperation. Didn't he have a right to know what had happened in his own past?

He could push her.

But would her face grow sad and drawn? Would it be worth upsetting her?

Better to throw myself into my work, he told himself. *And help out with the fencing.*

But why—*why*—wouldn't Mum answer him?

FENCE

Gulls cried raucously overhead, pivoting and wheeling and hanging in midair as if supervising the humans working on the beach. A line of village men stood waiting as Cyrus Hammer gave directions.

"Men, our fishing boats have reported a large enough number of mermaid sightings close to our shoreline that we're going ahead and fencing now even though it's a bit earlier than normal." His voice boomed noisily across the sand. Emerson was glad they were out in the open where the sound of the loud man's voice had room to dissipate. When he was in their cottage chatting with Emerson's mother, it seemed his conversational tone was almost too much for the walls to bear.

"Nobody knows enough about the mermaids and what triggers the Hunting Time to know why they're coming in early this year, but we're ready for them. As a side note, if anyone wants to make a scientific study of them, he's more than welcome." A ripple of laughter shook through the men. Nobody would ever be foolish enough.

At first Emerson thought perhaps Cyrus had been slyly referring to him. Then he remembered there was nothing whatsoever sly about the big man, and that he seemed barely aware of Emerson's existence most of the time. He relaxed.

"So!" Cyrus boomed. "We're going to work in pairs. Each pair will be responsible for putting up a 20 foot section of fence, so split up and get your supplies. First team to finish their section to my inspection gets a free round of drinks at Millie's on me!"

The assembled men cheered in response and scrambled to sort themselves into pairs.

"One more thing," Cyrus' voice called easily over the noise. "I don't need to remind you, but I am anyway. Stay out of the water!"

Emerson found himself paired with a fisherman named Ned. The man didn't speak much due to being hard of hearing. This was fine with Emerson since no conversation meant less attention drawn to him.

They were assigned the farthest end of the fence: the part that would butt up against the cliff near the Kadwell cottage.

They each dug down through the sand until they'd gotten to a more solid layer. Then they dug further. The fence posts would need to go four feet down to handle waves breaking against them when the tide was at its highest. Cyrus came and inspected the depth of the holes and nodded his approval.

Wordlessly, Emerson and Ned walked together to the pile of massive posts that had been dumped at the edge of the beach by a man driving an oxcart. The posts were 8 inches through and 9 feet long. Working together, they hoisted a beam onto their shoulders.

Emerson felt good being able to hold his own end without staggering. He may not be as burly as other lads his age who had been on fishing boats since their twelfth birthday, but he was no weakling. Ned gave him an approving nod when they successfully set the post into their first hole. Then it was back for another.

As they set the second post, Emerson's skin prickled. Someone was watching him. He glanced up, expecting to see Cyrus had arrived to inspect their work again. But he hadn't. Trying to appear casual, Emerson glanced along the width of the beach. Nobody was looking his way. He looked toward the Kadwell cottage. There were no windows facing him, so it couldn't be his mother.

*Maybe I **am** a little crazy,* he thought with a slight shudder.

He threw himself back into the job at hand. He and Ned pushed the wet sand they'd removed into the holes, packing it around the posts. The feeling of being watched never left him, and when he moved to fill in around the furthest post the feeling intensified.

He looked around again.

"Whatcha looking for?" Ned asked loudly.

"Nothing." Emerson ducked his head.

"What's that?" Ned said, cupping a hand around his "good" ear.

Emerson squirmed. The next team over was looking at them. *Great.*

Just then, a shout went up from a team further down the line. They had already finished their section. The other men groaned at the lost chance for a free round of drinks, but hurried to finish their own sections so they could join in before the fun at Millie's Pub was over.

"Sounds like they finished!" Ned said loudly. Apparently the cheer was loud enough for him to make out.

Emerson just nodded, thankful nobody was looking at him anymore. After a moment's hesitation, he stepped closer to Ned and spoke in a normal tone, but right next to the fisherman's "good" ear. "I just felt like someone was watching us for a minute there. You?"

The man shrugged. "Naw," he said loudly in Emerson's ear.

They were behind the other teams, but Ned didn't seem to mind. The last of the other men had headed to the village by the time they were nearly done.

At least Emerson didn't have to worry about attracting attention to himself when he shouted to Ned. "We're going to end up short a few slats!"

Ned surveyed their work and nodded. "Guess someone mis-counted how many to cut," he called.

"You go on," Emerson told him. "I'll cut some in my workshop and come nail them on."

Ned gave him a salute, "Thanks, lad!"

Emerson entered his cottage and found his mother knitting in her rocker. "How did it go?" she asked, looking up.

"Good, Mum! You should come see. Cyrus got everyone working extra fast by offering an incentive." He led her to the window that faced the sea.

Outside, the fence stretched five feet high across the entire width of the beach. It blocked the way to the water from one cliff to the other. The heavy posts stood upright and narrow slats were nailed horizontally between. The docks were inaccessible; the boats would lie at anchor until the Hunting Time was past.

"And the slats are close enough together to keep little children from slipping down to the water?" his mother asked.

He glanced at her sharply. "Yes. Cyrus made sure."

She nodded her approval. "Wouldn't want any of my little students wandering down there," she explained softly. As the village schoolteacher, she had a soft spot for all the little ones. Emerson knew she would feel terrible if anything happened to one of them.

He gestured to his section of the fence. "I need to make a few more slats for that side. I'll be in the workshop if you need anything."

An hour or so later, he'd finished planing some additional slats. He carefully maneuvered them through the cottage and out the front door.

When he rounded the side of the building and faced the sea, the feeling of being watched slammed into him with its full force. He had forgotten about it when he was inside.

But a quick glance around the deserted beach showed that he was alone.

HUNTING

Emerson shivered slightly. The feeling of being watched even though no one was on the shore made him want to turn around and go back inside the cottage. Unfortunately, his section of the fence would be unsafe without the slats he held. A child might slip down to the water during the Hunting Time unless the fence was full-height all the way across the beach.

He wouldn't be able to live with himself if one of the village children was taken by the mermaids, and he could have prevented it. The sailors' stories always sounded more like superstition and fairytales, but they were terrifying nevertheless.

Squaring his shoulders, Emerson continued forward. Suddenly, a terrible scream went up from somewhere around the fence. He fumbled the armful of slats and dropped them in a heap. The screaming turned to squawking and quick, rhythmic thumping.

It sounded like a gull.

Did mermaids hunt gulls?

Emerson didn't know. He crept closer to the fence, leaving his wooden slats on the sand. The thumping continued, the bird sounding extremely distressed. Nothing appeared to be disturbing the waves lapping on the shore beyond the fence.

Then he saw the bird: its head was caught between two fence slats a few sections to his right. Jogging through the sand, Emerson reached the spot quickly. The gull panicked even more, straining and beating its wings noisily against the wooden boards.

"You're going to snap your own neck if you don't calm down," Emerson said quietly.

One of the slats was cut unevenly to get around a knot in the wood. In that spot, the gap between the slats was narrower. Somehow—through typical gull curiosity and foolishness no doubt—the bird had slid its neck into this area.

Despite the fact that he could get pecked, scratched, or smacked in the face with a frenzied wing, Emerson decided he had to try to free the poor creature.

Glancing around and realizing he had nothing else useful with him, he stripped off his shirt. Praying his mother would understand if it got destroyed, he captured the beating wings and clawing feet in the white material, wrapping them tightly against the bird's body.

Keeping away from the beak, he slid the bird's neck to where the slats were further apart. The gull pulled its head free. Emerson released it quickly and jumped backward to avoid being attacked.

Launching into the air with a happy cry, the gull wheeled in a circle before joining the others further down the beach.

Emerson smiled. His shirt was not quite destroyed, but it would need some serious mending. He shrugged. At least he had escaped without a scratch and the bird was free.

Returning to his wood slats, he threw the shirt down next to them. The sea breeze was cool against his skin, but he didn't mind much. What made him more uncomfortable was that he felt eyes on him again.

I'm crazy. Touched in the head.

He shook his head and set about nailing the slats in place. He climbed partway up the fence to be at a better angle for nailing the topmost slat on. His hammer froze in mid-swing.

Something had moved in the corner of his eye. He climbed the rest of the way up and sat on the top of the fence. The waves lapped just a couple yards from him. Was that the movement he'd seen?

"Jumpy," he scolded himself under his breath.

He was about to climb down but decided to look at the waves just one more time.

Emerson squinted.

It was like a mirage. *An arm-shaped mirage.*

Just below the surface of the waves, a nearly transparent arm stretched forward toward him.

Mermaid!

Scrambling back to the far side of the fence, Emerson quickly pounding on the last slat. He stood for a moment, clutching his hammer as if it was a weapon. His mother would be terrified to hear of a mermaid trying to come up on the beach. He tried to remember if, in previous years, the mermaids had even come this close to the shore.

He resolved to keep the sighting to himself. Unless there were more. Then someone would need to be told.

Gathering his courage, he climbed up the fence near the very end where it butted up against the cliff wall. Steadying himself against the rock wall beside him, he stood on the topmost slat.

From this angle, he could see more than just the groping arm. Barely. The mermaid lay stretched on her stomach, one arm extended up the incline of the sand. No part of her seemed to break the surface of the water, as far as he could tell.

It was remarkably hard to see her. She was nearly as transparent as the water, and in the daylight her glow was invisible. With a quick movement, she pushed herself away from where the waves broke and into slightly deeper water.

Then she rolled over. Her appearance rippling and shimmering like a mirage in the waves. She opened her eyes and looked straight into Emerson's.

He recoiled and nearly fell off the fence. Wobbling to keep his balance, he looked back down at the water.

She stared unblinkingly and her mouth began to move as if she was speaking.

Just like in the stories. She's hunting... me.

TRAPPED

He couldn't breathe.
Water alternately pushed and pulled at him.
Suspended.
Straining.

WAKE UP, EMERSON!

His lungs burned and he wanted his mother.
A song. Music. Words.
Mother?
No, but a sea shanty she often sang over him.
Music in the water. Words.
Something pushing harder than the waves.

WAKE UP, EMERSON!

Sand.
Air.
Breath.
Mother.

Emerson finally pushed through the nightmare and up off his pillow. He gulped air. Somehow this time it felt more real, more terrifying. It was probably because now he knew it wasn't just a dream.

It was a snippet of memory.

He could feel that it was true, despite the fact that his mother wouldn't say.

Going to his bedroom window, he checked the sky. The stars told him it was just past midnight. He paced the room before deciding it felt more like a cage than anything.

Air. He always needed air after the nightmare.

Going through the familiar motions, he dressed and stole quietly out of the house. The night air was much warmer than it had been a couple nights ago when he'd last snuck out. He climbed the steep path to the top of the cliff and walked slowly toward the edge.

A tiny sliver of a moon hung low in the sky, and the dark waves were punctuated by half a dozen blueish glows. The mermaids were closing in on the island of Azul. They had put up the fence not a moment too soon. Emerson sat at the edge of the cliff and drooped.

Would the nightmare ever stop returning? Why did it plague him?

Emerson buried his hands deep in his unruly black hair. He willed himself not to listen for a familiar sea shanty in the noise of the waves.

"The sea does **not** sing!" he shouted above the noise.

But it had.

Knowing that, at some level, the dream was a memory made the whole thing more maddening. *How do I have a memory of the sea singing?*

Seconds turned into minutes and minutes stretched on. Emerson still sat, staring toward the sea, but seeing nothing. He was turning over possible reasons for the dream to occur tonight of all nights.

Perhaps it was a response to being down on the beach. He had spent most of the previous day working on the fence. He had been within a few yards of the lapping water for hours.

And he had seen a mermaid.

The thought jolted him. He lay down on his stomach and crept forward toward the crumbling edge of the cliff. Gripping the rocks so tightly his knuckles turned white, he peered over the edge.

Almost straight below him, a blue glow punctuated the shallows.

In the darkness, he could see the mermaid much more clearly. She was young—perhaps younger than he was—and her hair seemed to be dark. She was clearly of mixed parentage like so many in the island chain. She had the large, dark eyes of native Cayan women. Her skin, however, was pale. So pale. She wore a simple white gown that swirled around her legs in the moving water.

Emerson blinked and looked closer. Some claimed mermaids had fish tails in place of legs and feet. This one certainly didn't. She had small, very human feet.

Emerson glanced back up to her face. This time, she wasn't looking at him. She was lying on her side, looking at something next to her and doing something with her hands. The glow around her illuminated the water just enough that he could make out a dark shape—a rock if he had his guess.

The mermaid pushed on it frantically. It didn't budge.

Emerson cocked his head, confused as to why she was trying to move the large rock. He looked closer. She was curled up in a sort of hollowed-out place, ringed in by low rocks on three sides and the one large rock on the left.

Then she did something that shocked him. She reached up and placed her hand flat against the *underside* of the surface of the water—as if it was a ceiling—and pushed against it to roll herself.

How?!

She pulled herself forward toward the low rocks.

"If I didn't know better, I'd say she looks like she's trying to squeeze through a narrow opening," Emerson said to himself as he watched her try to maneuver between the rocks and the surface of the water.

She's trapped, he realized. *No one has ever seen a mermaid surface because... they can't surface.*

He sat back from the edge of the cliff, trying to understand what he had just discovered. After a moment he jumped to his feet and dashed down the path. When he arrived at the base of the cliff, he scrambled over the fence and plunged toward the water.

It's a good thing nobody can see me.

If the mermaid couldn't break out of the water, that meant he could safely help free her as long as he wasn't in the water where she could reach him!

MEMORY

Emerson kept clear of the waves as he ran to where the mermaid's light glowed. He circled around to the side where the large rock was hemming her in. Taking a deep breath, he removed his boots and socks before wading into the waves. By the time he reached the rock, the water level was up to his knees, and he'd had to roll up the legs of his trousers.

He looked down into the water at the beautiful, glowing creature just a few feet away. With the rock between them and her unable to surface, he was technically safe. Still, his heart hammered in his chest.

What a fool he was for intentionally getting this close to a mermaid! They should have made the fence high enough to keep 17-year-old young men away, apparently.

The mermaid rolled again, startling him. Her eyes widened when she saw him. The hammering in his chest increased and he fought to maintain control over his breathing.

Her mouth moved—though no sound reached his ears—, and she gestured to the large rock.

"I know," Emerson said without thinking. "I think I can move it if you push too."

To his shock she nodded eagerly.

She can hear me but I can't hear her?

"Will you hurt me if I help you?" Emerson ventured to ask.

She shook her head violently and mouthed something that looked like "No."

Here goes nothing.

Emerson found a grip on the rock and dug his heels into the wet sand beneath him. "Push!" he grunted.

On the other side of the rock, the mermaid pushed against it with her feet. It budged ever so slightly. He repositioned his own feet and shoved again, harder.

This time, the rock moved forward a few inches, sluggish in the wet sand. Rocking forward and digging in with his toes, Emerson gave one last heave, feeling the muscles in his arms bulge.

The rock rolled and disappeared beneath the surface of the water. Backing out of the waves quickly, Emerson looked over at the mermaid. She tried to squeeze through the opening made when the rock shifted. It wasn't quite large enough. She was still trapped.

She looked at him pleadingly.

After a moment's deliberation, Emerson waded back into the water. He felt around with his hands until he found a good grip on the submerged rock.

Bracing himself once again, he gave a mighty shove. In an instant, the rock dropped away and he felt his feet slip over the edge of—something.

Blazes! A shelf!

Emerson had the presence of mind to take a big gulp of air a second before he was completely submerged. He fought off the panic that screamed he was reliving his nightmare.

The real terror was the fact that he was sinking through dark water with a mermaid yards away. He twisted around and realized she was indeed free now.

And she was coming straight toward him.

Hunting Time.

Emerson tried to swim away, but she was far faster than he was—unnaturally so. She caught him by the arm and tried to pull him closer to her.

He thrashed and jerked away, propelling himself deeper into the depths.

Quick as a flash, she was behind him, pinning his arms to his sides in an eerily glowing embrace. Emerson began twisting and kicking.

All at once he froze.

Long we've tossed on the rolling main, now we're safe ashore, Jack.

The song. It was the song.

Emerson slowly turned his head to look at the girl holding him tightly against her as she swam strongly toward the shore.

She smiled at him and sang another line, her voice sweet and high.

Don't forget your old shipmate, faldee raldee raldee raldee rye-eye-doe!

"You can hear me, then?" she asked.

It was his turn to nod mutely just before she pushed him upward and he took a gasping breath of sea air. He was back on the sandy bottom above the shelf, pulling himself forward on hands and knees and breathing gratefully.

He sat down in the waves and stared into the water where the glowing girl floated just below. And he didn't feel afraid in the slightest.

"You can hear me, right?" he said a little uncertainly.

She nodded, smiling broadly.

"Thank you for rescuing me," he said. "I feel like maybe we've had the wrong idea about you all along."

She cocked her head and beckoned to him.

Emerson regarded her uncertainly for a moment. She tossed her head and beckoned again, this time cupping her ear.

Oh, of course. He realized he would have to put his head under the water to hear her.

Taking a deep breath, he did.

"Thank you for rescuing *me*," she said in her sweet voice. "The tide went out and with the lower water level, I was trapped among the rocks. I didn't think it through—I was so busy watching for you."

Emerson pulled his head out of the water and said, "You were watching for me?"

She nodded.

"We've met before, haven't we." He ducked back under the water.

"Yes," she said. "You were just a wee one. You toddled down here and fell in before your mother had noticed you were gone. I caught you and pushed you back to shore. I sang to you to keep you calm."

Tears sprang to Emerson's eyes before he could stop them. *The sea didn't sing to me: a mermaid did!*

The girl looked like she had more to say, so he popped up for another breath and then submerged himself again.

Her eyes were profoundly sad as she said, "You all *have* had the wrong idea about us. And I'm afraid the truth is more terrible than the sailors' lore."

MERMAIDS

Emerson pulled his head out of the water. This was such a strange way of communicating, but mermaids were strange creatures, so he supposed it wasn't that surprising.

His mind was already working out ways to make the communication easier. If the mermaid's story was a long one, he would have to keep interrupting her to sit up and take a new breath.

At least I'm not panicking from holding my breath underwater! he realized with a jolt. That in itself was a miracle.

"I have an idea," he said to the glowing girl waiting just beneath the waves. "Stay right there; I'll be back in a moment."

He dashed up the beach, his feet slipping and churning sand. The cool breeze plastered his wet clothes to him, but he ignored it. He quickly climbed over the fence and headed toward the path that wound up the cliff.

The moonlight was just bright enough for him to make out a stand of reeds growing near the path.

Working mostly by feel in the dimness, he selected a reed he felt was a sufficient size and sturdiness.

Hurrying back over the top of the fence and down to the water, he splashed into the waves.

To his relief, the mermaid still waited. She looked glad that he had returned as well.

"I got a reed!" he said excitedly as soon as he was touching the water. He had realized the water somehow carried the sound of their voices between them.

She raised an eyebrow questioningly.

Amazing that she can be so expressive with her face, even though she's semi-transparent, he thought.

"It's so I can breathe while listening to you. Less interruptions," he explained.

Understanding dawned on her face and she smiled.

Emerson fitted the reed into his mouth and ducked under the surface, keeping it upright as he did so. Sure enough: he could breathe through the hollow center.

"That's ingenious, lad," the mermaid said.

Emerson sat right up out of the water and took the reed out of his mouth. "Lad? Surely you're not *that* much older than me! Also, my name is Emerson."

Replacing the reed and submerging again, he was surprised to see the mermaid's expression had turned exceedingly sad. He was about to sit up again and apologize for whatever it was he'd said.

But she anticipated his intention and waved her hand. "No, no, stay. Please don't apologize, Emerson. You are most certainly not the one at fault. My name is Lilyse, and I am at the same time 15 and 35 years old."

It was Emerson's turn to be puzzled. Her name was beautiful and suited her perfectly, but what was this about her age?

Lilyse sighed deeply and stared down at the sand shifting beneath them as it sloped away toward the deep sea. After a moment, she looked up at him. Emerson was shocked to see tears rolling down her face.

Why aren't her tears just mixing with the water? It's almost like she's not really here.

"Now that I finally get to tell someone the truth, I don't even know how to begin," she whispered. Emerson waited. "I lived on Stron Cay with my mother."

Emerson sat up out of the water. *So much for less interruptions!* "You mean you live in one of the harbors? Or in the general waters around Stron Cay?"

"No," Lilyse said when he was back under the surface. "I used to live *on* the island itself. I lived in a small village inland with my mother. I never knew my father, but Mother and I worked hard and made a decent life for ourselves. One day, representatives of Shaman Orith came to our village. They said the lot for the Sea Appeasement had fallen on our village and the Shaman would arrive the next day to finalize the selection."

Emerson had heard much of Shaman Orith. The man was a bit of a legend as leader of the island chain's ritualistic religion. He primarily held sway over the main island, Stron Cay, but he was known throughout the other islands as well, where he continually tried to spread his influence.

Just as the islands' populations were a mixture of native Cayans and newcomers living side by side, there were followers of Shaman Orith and his pantheon of magical gods, and people who believed in one god called Omega.

Many sailors found it convenient to combine bits of both religions. They said they worshiped Omega, but also held to the idea of the Sea as a god they needed to be on good terms with. Emerson had never seen how one could logically hold to both religions at the same time, though.

Lilyse spoke of appeasing the sea as if it was a well-known ritual, but this wasn't something he'd heard of before. Perhaps it was common on Stron Cay?

"Shaman Orith and his men arrived early the next morning. They carried the Shaman into the center of our village on a covered litter.

"Nobody from my village had ever seen him. Everyone crowded around curiously. The more devout followers did a lot of bowing and kneeling. They drew back the curtains and there he was. He wore a long red robe with a large hood drawn up over his head. He was darker, like a native Cayan, but I could see his beard was red like some of the settlers.

"It was all very mysterious and the crowd fell silent, wondering what would happen next."

Lilyse paused and shivered. "He looked coldly around, and then he raised a hand and pointed to me, standing near my mother at the edge of the crowd. 'She is the one,' he said in a low, hoarse voice. His followers took me from my mother, who had begun to cry. They told her because of me the Sea would be appeased and sailors would be safer, catches larger, storms less severe.

"They put me on a horse and we left the village quickly. I don't remember much—it was all such a blur—, but we journeyed the rest of the day before reaching the Shaman's village on the north coast of Stron Cay.

"They put me in a hut down on the beach overnight, guarded closely.

"The next morning, someone threw in a white dress for me to change into. Nobody bothered to feed me, but instead hurried me straight onto a waiting boat. The entire population of the Shaman's village came out onto the beach cheering and chanting.

"We sailed north a ways before they dropped the anchor."

Lilyse had tears rolling down her face again. "The Shaman recited a strange chant about the Sea," her light voice continued. "I cannot forget the last line: 'And blessed Sea, receive from our hand this pure sacrifice.'"

Emerson's eyes widened as horrified understanding dawned over him. He sat up quickly and spit out the reed. "They threw you overboard? You were a sacrifice to supposedly appease the Sea?"

She nodded sadly, and he smacked the water with his hand. *How was this okay?*

"But something must have happened... how did you become a mermaid?" he asked when he was finally ready to hear the rest of the story. He ducked back under the water.

"Something did happen. I died."

If he hadn't been underwater, Emerson's mouth would have dropped open.

"You may call me a mermaid, but in reality I am a ghost. I am water-bound because I was killed unjustly in the water. It's been 20 years."

Emerson sat up. Lilyse just looked at him, waiting. He felt like he should be shocked or afraid that she was a ghost, but the horror of her murder outweighed that feeling.

This beautiful girl—a girl who saved my life—was killed as a sacrifice.

A thought dawned on him as he looked out to sea. "And the others?" He ducked under to hear her reply.

"There are 30 of us. One for each year. And, Emerson? We need your help. We believe that when Shaman Orith is brought to justice we will be freed to rest in peace."

TRUTH

Emerson stared listlessly out his bedroom window. He was so tired he was beginning to see double. He hadn't slept at all after talking with Lilyse.

Who could?

How was Shaman Orith getting away with murdering innocent girls? How did the adherents to his religion make their peace with such a thing? How did the girls' parents just give them up?

Emerson's mind had been swirling with questions and no answers since he'd trudged back to the house. He had thrown his wet clothes on the floor of his room and burrowed under the quilt.

Only to stare at the small window until it grew grey, then pink, then golden.

His mother was fixing breakfast; he could hear the pans clanking and her soft humming. He heard a quiet knock—but not on his bedroom door.

"Emrie, love, breakfast is ready."

She must think he had been shut in his workshop since before she got up. He did that sometimes.

With a sigh, he slid out of bed and pulled on his now-dry clothes. They were crisp with dried salt water, but he didn't care.

He opened his bedroom door, and his mother turned in surprise. "Why, there you are! Are you feeling well? I thought you were up working already."

He tried to paint his face with a relaxed and neutral expression. "I'm good."

She puckered her eyebrows but didn't say anything further about it.

Rather than heading to the small table, Emerson went to the bookcases lining one wall of the cottage's main area. His mother, being the village schoolteacher, collected books on a wide range of topics. She had let him read them freely from the moment he could string sounds together into words. He had read most, but not all, of her collection.

"What are you looking for?" she asked, spooning hot oats into two bowls.

"This one," Emerson said, darting forward for a large volume on the bottom shelf. He sat crosslegged on the floor and pulled it into his lap. Pushing his hair out of his eyes, he opened the massive volume and flipped through it quickly.

"*An Encyclopedic History of The Cayan Islands*?" his mother asked.

"Mmhm," he murmured, barely hearing her.

He had found the article on the native religion. Reading quickly, he took in the whole entry—customs, beliefs, superstitions, their odd use of seaweed in producing magic—before the second time his mother mentioned his food was getting cold. Closing the volume with a thud, he shelved it and stood.

Nothing about human sacrifice. It's never been a part of the religion. Even on Stron Cay, the main island...

His face wore a thoughtful expression and his mother left him in peace while he tried to eat. She was used to, and respectful of, his bookish and often distracted ways.

After a while, his mother approached. "You're not eating, Emrie."

"Hmm? Oh." He glanced down at the barely touched bowl of congealing oats.

"I—" he looked up and stopped when he saw his mother's face. She was staring at his pant legs with a mixture of fear and disbelief. He followed her gaze and saw the unmistakeable salt stains that sea water left behind.

"Emerson!" she breathed, looking up at his face. "You've been in the water!"

He hadn't planned to tell her.

Yet.

Like this.

"Mum—"

"During the *Hunting Time*?" her face had reddened with expanding emotion and her eyes were filling with unshed tears.

"But the *Hunting Time* isn't what we've thought. They're not hunting! Mum! The mermaids aren't mermaids at all!"

"'The mermaids aren't mermaids at all!' What do you think you're even saying, Emerson? You've never been one to lie to me or make excuses. We've never had a relationship like that, but lately... I don't know, son." She gasped with what should have been a sob if she'd not been trying to hold it in so hard.

Emerson jumped to his feet and took his mother's hands. "Mum," he said softly, his voice cracking. "I'm sorry to have worried you, but please—please?—hear me out. This is going to sound crazy but it will explain what's going on and that I haven't been in any real danger."

His mother shook her head, but she let him seat her at the table. He returned to his chair across from her and pondered where to begin.

"Mum, I've talked to a mermaid named Lilyse." He winced as her mouth dropped open and she threw her hands into the air. "I know it sounds crazy, but you know me: I discovered how to converse with them.

"Listen. She was trapped when the tide went out, so I found a way to help her without being in danger. The mermaids never surface because they *can't*. The surface of the water is literally like a ceiling to her. I made sure she couldn't get to me.

"And, Mum, when something did happen and I fell into deeper water, she—she rescued me!"

"No!" his mother cried, burying her face in her hands. "No, don't say that! Who told you that?"

Emerson squinted his eyes, confused. "Mum, when I was shoving the rock that was trapping her, I fell off a shelf and into deep water. I was terrified because she was loose and I was in the water, but she grabbed hold of me and pulled me back up to the shore.

"She saved me, and then we talked. If I'm touching the water in any way, she can hear me when I speak. If I put my head under the water, I can hear her."

His mother had begun shaking her head. *She doesn't believe me.*

"Mum! I swear I'm telling the truth! This all just happened last night!" They were silent for a moment. Finally, Emerson spoke again. "When I was a toddling baby, I wandered down to the shallows and fell in. I was drowning. I still have nightmares about it. I was under for what felt like an eternity. Lilyse found me and brought me back to the shore, pushing me back up onto the sand the best she could.

"She sang a sea shanty to calm me, Mum, and I still hear it in my dreams. You found me face up on the sand. You might have seen her, but since she's nearly transparent in the daylight you dismissed it as a trick of the eye."

His mother had gone perfectly calm and was staring at him, one hand over her mouth.

"How do you know all that?" she said in a breathless whisper.

"Doesn't it make you wonder, Mum? Since you and Father never spoke a word of it to me and my nightmares have been a muddled version of it."

"She—she told you."

Emerson nodded solemnly, trying to gauge just how much his mother believed him.

"But even if this mermaid didn't hurt you and instead saved your life—twice from the sound of it— what was so important that you stayed? In the water? At night? During the Hunting Time?" She looked worried and still slightly skeptical.

"She was telling me about the mermaids and asking for help on their behalf. Because, Mum, they're not mermaids—" Emerson stopped and stared at his hands. Would the truth be too much of a shock to his mother's already frayed nerves? "They're ghosts, actually." He said, glancing up at her earnestly.

His mother sat back in her chair abruptly and stared.

"They're the water-bound ghosts of girls Shaman Orith has been sacrificing to the Sea this time each year. They believe they will finally rest if he is brought to justice."

"Emerson, you can't tell anyone about this!" his mother gasped. "Everyone will think you're touched in the head, and it's sure to reach the Shaman's ears that you're accusing him of murder!"

"Son, are you worrying your mother again?" boomed a shockingly loud voice. Emerson jumped out of his chair with all the grace of a startled rabbit.

Cyrus Hammer stood in the open doorway.

How much did he hear? And why *the blazes does he insist on calling me that?*

DECISIONS

Emerson leaned over his workbench, his hands deftly selecting the tools he would need. The invention had been forming in his mind since the moment he had figured out how to communicate with Lilyse.

He would create a tube: like a listening horn, but with both ends flared and a membrane over one end. He had a theory that the membrane would transfer the sound from the water into the tube and then to his ear.

He would need to run down to the water and test it, but not until that obnoxious man, Cyrus, decided to finally leave their cottage. He glanced in annoyance toward the closed door of the workshop.

Cyrus' loud voice boomed through from the kitchen, invading his quiet space and his thoughts. "Idina, the boy can't be serious! He convinced you by describing something you had never told him about? Does it occur to you that someone else could have told him?"

His mother's soft voice answered, "I thought of that, Mr. Hammer, but most of the villagers only know he nearly drowned when he was 17 months old. They don't know the specifics of how I found him or what he's been having nightmares about since that time!"

"Regardless! It's preposterous, not to mention insane to think he sat and had a chat with a mermaid."

"You think he dreamt the whole thing?"

"I do, Idina. And I hope for your sake that's the case."

"Then, Mr. Hammer, how do you explain the salt water stains all over his clothes: the very clothes I washed just yesterday?"

Emerson heard the sound of a fist slamming into the kitchen table and he almost jumped to the door. But Cyrus' next words sounded frustrated, not dangerous. "Then we have to assume he did go down to the water. But that leaves us with two bad scenarios: either he is intentionally deceiving you, or he is truly touched in the head as the village gossips like to claim.

"Either option is very bad for you, my Idina."

Hearing Cyrus call his mother "his" made Emerson ball his fists and stride to the closed door faster than even the fist on the table had.

His mother's voice stopped him in his tracks. "Those are not the only two scenarios. My boy and I have the kind of relationship many parents and children never have. We are friends and have no secrets—beyond the one about his accident. And I'm more and more ashamed I kept that one from him.

"I trust my boy implicitly, Mr. Hammer. I'm not saying you have to, but know that's where I stand on the topic."

Emerson swallowed a lump in his throat and relaxed his hands. She believed him. And she seemed to have her annoying visitor well in hand.

Good on you, Mum.

She hadn't flown off the handle even once—which was more than he could say for his handling of his own annoying visitor: Saria.

He shook his head. Perhaps such people were a part of everyone's life, and he should take a cue from his mother on how to respond.

He went back to his workbench and the beginnings of his communication device.

He wasn't sure exactly what to do about Lilyse and the other mermaids, but he did know being able to communicate more easily with her was going to be important. He'd put in the work to figure something out.

"Idina, I see I can't change your mind—at least not yet, but let me ask this: how do you plan to keep this delusion—or whatever it is—under wraps? You simply *can't* let the villagers know about this.

"Why, you'll be a laughingstock, and if the governor hears he might even reconsider your post as schoolteacher!"

"And it would be worth it, Mr. Hammer, if the murder of innocent Cayan girls were to be stopped as a result. Don't you think?" his mother asked primly.

The governor.

Emerson hadn't even thought of this. Governor Aldan could get in touch with the governor of Stron Cay who would then be obligated to begin an investigation. He would quickly discover that human sacrifice wasn't something normally part of the religion and was something that Shaman Orith had invented for his own unknown, vile purposes...

Emerson put down his tools and stared into space for a moment before taking a deep breath. That was what he needed to do. He needed to see Governor Aldan and tell him the truth about the mermaids.

For all his loud and obnoxious protestations, Cyrus was right about one thing: the whole village— no, the whole island—might find out if his story went beyond the walls of the cottage.

His heart squeezed in fear of being that laughingstock the man had mentioned. His breathing sped up, and he took a few moments to slow it back down. Now was not a good time for losing control.

Saving himself from embarrassment or stopping the murders of innocent girls? Suddenly, his path was very clear.

Telling the authorities was the right thing to do. That's all there was to it.

He swallowed hard and put his hand on the doorknob.

DETERMINATION

Emerson's mother and Cyrus Hammer looked up when he pulled the door open. His mother seemed to suddenly realize he had been able to hear Cyrus' loud voice from the workshop, for her face softened into a concerned expression.

"Hi," Emerson said feeling a little less sure of himself now that they were both staring at him.

Isn't this always my problem? People staring at me doesn't change what's right. It doesn't change what's right.

He took a deep breath. "Mum, I've made a decision."

Cyrus frowned. His mother cocked her head and turned to face Emerson fully.

"I'm going to get in touch with the authorities. If the mermaid's story is accurate, there's a great crime being committed on Stron Cay, and the governors should know about it. They can bring Shaman Orith to justice. Then no more girls will be sacrificed, and the mermaids can finally rest in peace." His stomach clenched as he said it.

Cyrus rose to his feet. "That is a terrible idea. I'm not sure what is going on with you, but no matter what it is, you should be able to see that this fanciful story will bring shame and trouble to your mother."

The big man tried to soften his growl and was mostly unsuccessful. "You're a good lad to your mother as she was just explaining, so I know you don't often do things this foolish."

"So you're saying allowing murders to continue just to keep some stupid villagers from talking is a good idea?" Emerson said hotly. Making up his mind to be this bold had been hard enough, he couldn't let Cyrus talk him out of it.

"No," Cyrus boomed, gesturing with his hands, "what I'm saying is that you are possibly lying or out of your mind, and I will allow neither to stain your mother's reputation and standing in this community!"

"Oh, you won't *allow* it?" Emerson said quietly, taking a step forward. "What gives you the right to allow or disallow anything? The same thing that gives you the right to drop into our lives and our cottage without any kind of invitation?"

Cyrus straightened and his eyes sparked with anger. "You have no right to speak to me like that. You're not going to the governor, son, and that's final."

Emerson clenched his fists and said in a low voice. "You, Cyrus, are not—and never will be—my father. So if you would stop calling me *son* and show yourself out of our cottage immediately, I would be much obliged."

Out of the corner of his eye, Emerson noticed his mother quirk a smile. She was proud of him lowering his voice rather than escalating things further.

Cyrus growled. "You little cur! I know a good woman like your mother must have taught you some manners at some point. Manners like speaking respectfully to your elders. You're completely out of line ordering me around. I'll leave whenever the blazes I'm ready! And not just because a bookish little sob like yourself gave me an order."

"That's enough!" Idina pushed between them, nearly glowing with anger. "You will NOT speak like that in my house, Cyrus Hammer. When my husband died, my son became man of the house, and as he's asked you to leave you've far, *far* overstayed your welcome by still remaining."

She drew herself up to her tallest height, which was still tiny compared to the man's bulk.

He seemed to snap out of it, however, and the redness began to recede from his face. "I do hope you realize I'm only trying to help you, Idina. Good day."

He left, letting the door close none too gently behind him.

Emerson stole a glance at his mother. She was trembling with what he assumed to be fright. While annoying and seemingly ever-present, Cyrus Hammer had never shown anger before.

"It's okay, Mum. He's gone, and he'll hopefully be less meddlesome in the future." He gave her a hug.

She laughed shakily from inside his embrace. "You think I'm scared? No, Emerson Kadwell, I'm angrier than I think I've ever been. To see him sit under my roof and shame my son right in front of me. The way he disrespected me and then you—my word."

Emerson looked down at his mother in surprise. She had never expressed much of an opinion of 'Mr. Hammer' as she insisted on calling him. She had politely put up with his frequent visits and his obvious, if awkward, interest in her.

"He's not always this bad," he pointed out.

"Just almost," she whispered with an improper giggle.

Emerson grinned.

His mother grew solemn. "I believe if you go to Governor Aldan it will very likely cause trouble for us." For the first time since making his decision, Emerson felt a wave of doubt. But then his mother continued. "But Emrie, I completely agree that it's the right thing to do."

She brushed his hair back from his forehead and gave him a tight, but approving smile. His heart swelled at her words, but he wished it would do more to loosen the knot in his stomach.

GOVERNOR

Emerson covered a yawn with the back of his hand. He had been up long before the sun, throwing a few things into his satchel and setting off on foot for Primus, the main town on the north side of Azul.

He had managed to ride a few times with people headed the same direction: once in an oxcart, once in a messenger's chariot, and once on the second horse a kind man was leading behind his own.

Still, by the time he arrived in the large town, he was beginning to feel just how long he had been awake. There was very little he could do at the moment, since he'd put in a request to speak with Governor Aldan. The governor's secretary had jotted down his name, village, and the summary, "Information on a possible crime."

He had then told Emerson to have a seat to wait until his turn in the queue.

That had been over 2 hours ago, according to the ornate mechanical clock on the wall. It was mid-afternoon, and he realized at this point there was very little hope of him making it back home the same day.

The small entry room in which he waited was warm and stuffy from the dozen or so other people waiting for an audience. The man they all waited to see sat somewhere beyond beautiful oak doors in an office attached to the Governor's Mansion.

There was very little discussion among the people waiting. The warmth seemed to be making everyone a bit sleepy. What little talk there was had begun to turn from restlessness to grumbling.

Emerson tuned them out and covered another yawn.

I sure hope I'm not mid-yawn when the secretary comes for me.

Just then, the oak doors swung open to expel a frowning woman. Her interview had obviously not gone as she'd hoped. The secretary followed her out, consulting his list.

"His Excellency Governor Aldan will now see Emerson Kadwell of Chadwick village." He glanced up over the rim of his spectacles as if wondering whether the person he had called was still there.

Emerson had already jumped to his feet, clutching his satchel. He found he was gripping it far more tightly than necessary.

"Very good, right this way, lad."

They stepped through the doors, and Emerson stopped halfway across the room. The secretary continued forward and went to stand at the elbow of the bored-looking man sitting behind a heavy desk.

"Your Excellency, this is Emerson Kadwell of Chadwick village with information on a possible crime," the secretary read dutifully.

"Hmm," said the governor, giving Emerson a dubious once-over. "Chadwick's a fishing village. Lots of sailors and such, but you're so pale. Sick are you?"

The secretary started and looked up nervously, as if wondering whether he should have inquired about this before allowing Emerson inside.

"N-no sir." Emerson found his voice. "I don't work on a fishing boat. I repair things in my workshop and—well, I invent new things when I have the time."

"Hmm." Governor Aldan raised his brows as if straining to keep his half-lidded eyes open at all. "And what's this about a possible crime? Someone stealing fish?"

Emerson cleared his throat and prayed it wouldn't crack or warble. He had been beyond that stage for a couple years, but in these circumstances... anything could happen. "More like stealing life, sir."

The governor tipped his head to one side. "I'm listening."

"Well, sir—the mermaids. See, I've talked to one, and—"

Governor Aldan interrupted with a snort. Emerson paused. "Oh, do go on," the man said, "this is bound to be the most entertainment I've had all day."

Emerson's cheeks heated, but he continued doggedly. "I figured out how to talk to one and she

81

DENVER EVANS

told me their story. They're not mermaids at all, sir, but ghosts bound to the water they were unjustly killed in."

The governor leaned his head to the other side, staring hard at Emerson. It seemed as if he was trying to decide whether Emerson was pranking him or crazy.

"I know it sounds hard to believe, sir, but I'm telling you exactly what I heard. Apparently, for the last 30 years, Shaman Orith has been offering girls as appeasement sacrifices to the sea. Until he's brought to justice they will continue to be trapped in the water, unable to find rest."

Emerson fell silent. The governor cocked his head back and exchanged glances with his secretary. The other man wore a tired look.

The leather of the governor's chair creaked as he sat forward and rested his elbows on his desk. His former boredom had been replaced with a sternness that seemed to be chiseled into his face.

"Without more to go on than the second-hand report of what a sea creature supposedly said, it would be completely foolish of me to bother Governor Milus of Stron Cay about this matter. And to be frank, you shouldn't be wasting my time with this."

Emerson frowned. *He's being condescending. And he thinks I'm crazy.*

"Sir—"

"Enough!" growled Governor Aldan, smacking his palm against the desk top. "Do not remonstrate with me—if you even know the meaning of the word!

You're a half-wit who stands here taking up my time with suspicions and groundless claims against a well-respected man."

Emerson's heart rate accelerated.

The governor added in a quiet voice. "If this is the kind of fool your mother has raised, I cannot begin to imagine what kind of education she's giving the children of Chadwick. Don't make me regret her installation as schoolteacher."

This stopped Emerson's heart entirely. He had to get out of there.

SEMAPHORE

Emerson ran from the steps of the Governor's Mansion and bent over in a deserted alley where he promptly got sick.

The man did not just disbelieve me, he threatened my mother's livelihood.

He hoped the threats were empty. If not, he would do everything in his power to provide for her.

When the aching in his chest had subsided and he had succeeded in regulating his breathing, Emerson left the alley and slipped through the streets.

A mounted messenger galloped past him on his way out of the city. After that, he had an illogical fear that someone from the mansion was just behind him. That they would notice him and say, "Stop, boy! We forgot to remove your mother as schoolteacher! Here, carry this letter home to her."

Just on the outskirts of town, a horse and cart caught up to him. He kept his head low and moved to the left so it would pass.

But it didn't. The cart pulled up alongside him and stopped. A familiar voice said, "Emerson?"

No. Not her!

Not here! Not now!

Emerson glanced up. The Beggleys' housekeeper sat in the front of a small cart, holding the reins. Saria sat in the back, wearing something ruffled and pale blue, a straw hat tied on with a white scarf. She smiled.

"It *is* you! I wasn't sure for a moment—it's confusing to see someone you know in a place you'd never expect! What are you doing here?"

Emerson's mouth twitched. He wasn't sure how to answer.

"Hold on just a moment, Madge," Saria said, stepping down from the cart. "Actually, let's not block the road with that thing. Go ahead and drive outside the town. Emerson and I will walk that way and join you in a moment."

The housekeeper clucked to the horses, and the cart pulled away, leaving Emerson standing in the middle of the road with the last person he was hoping to see.

Second to last, he reminded himself. *I'd rather not see Governor Aldan again right now.*

He looked quickly back the way he'd come.

"What's wrong, Emerson?" Saria asked, laying a hand briefly on his arm. "Are you in some kind of trouble?"

They began walking again, and Emerson tried to figure out what to say.

Finally, as the edge of the town melted into a hayfield, he said, "I just came to speak with someone."

"And it didn't go well?"

Well, I was trying to leave that part out, but since you seem so determined to embarrass me—

"Yes—no. It didn't."

"I'm sorry," she said, turning to look at him with a million questions still swirling around her face.

For the first time he could remember, Emerson felt gratitude toward Saria for something. She didn't ask any more questions.

"I came to Primus to visit my aunt two days ago. Father says I need to spend time around a woman more. Apparently without a mother I'm in danger of becoming a drunken, bearded sailor..."

Emerson snorted and glanced over to find her eyes twinkling with amusement. She was rather pretty when she wasn't tormenting him.

"Look out, Emerson!" she said suddenly. He hadn't been watching where he was walking. He swerved just in time to avoid colliding with a farmer standing in the middle of the road. The man had halted and was staring at something behind them. Curious, Emerson and Saria turned as well.

Above the town loomed a tower. At its top, the semaphore telegraph used to send messages to the neighboring islands of Stron Cay and Miren, was slowly swinging through its positions. The arms moved, paused, moved, and paused again.

"He's doing it!" Emerson whispered, unable to believe what he was seeing. "He's really sending a message to Stron Cay!"

"Who? What?" Saria was looking at him, puzzled.

"Maybe my meeting with the—maybe it didn't go as badly as I thought. He's actually signaling Stron Cay!" Emerson stared at the moving arms, wishing he knew the semaphore alphabet. He wondered if any of his mother's books had information on it.

Saria touched his arm again, making him jump. "What?" he said, startling out of his thoughts.

"Would you like a ride home?"

Emerson's legs screamed "YES!" He eyed the cart stopped along the road just ahead of them. If he accepted her offer, he would get home just before dark.

"You can tell me more about why you were meeting with the governor!" Saria said brightly.

Emerson's heart lurched. *How does she know that? Probably because the governor is the one who would order the semaphore into motion, you fool!* "No, thanks. I'm not in the mood for an interrogation," he said sharply before walking away as briskly as he dared.

Yes, he wanted to get as far away from her prying as he could, but he certainly didn't want to look like he was running away from a girl!

Especially one who couldn't be trusted not to go home and spread rumors.

ANGER

Emerson had stopped to catch a bit of sleep sometime long after midnight. He found shelter in a barn and left before it was light. His legs ached bitterly from walking all the way to and from Primus in one 24-hour period.

He tried not to think about how he'd be waking up in his own bed right then if only he'd taken Saria's offer to ride back to Chadwick in her cart.

Bleary-eyed, he crested a small rise and found himself looking down at the village of Chadwick just being touched by newborn rays of sun. Beyond, the sea sparkled blindingly in the sunrise.

Dragging himself the last little way, he entered the village. People were already up and around in the pale morning.

It's good to be back, he thought. *Primus is just too big for my liking. Chadwick, even, is too busy sometimes. But it does feel like home even if I've always lived on the outskirts.*

A woman walked past and gave him a wide berth, furrowing her brows and looking him up and down.

He didn't blame her. *I probably look awful.*

But when he passed a small group of men and their conversation immediately halted to watch him with wary eyes, he began to wonder. A prickling sensation crept up his neck and he looked around.

Everyone was noticing him. And it wasn't in a good way.

Two older women put their heads together, whispering behind their hands. They shook their heads, looking at him disapprovingly.

Somehow, the entire village knew something.

As he passed one of the houses, someone grabbed his arm and jerked him inside.

Someone strong.

"Um, hello, Cyrus."

"Emerson Kadwell! What have you done?"

"I—I'm not sure. People are acting strangely. At first I thought I was imagining it," Emerson stuttered.

Cyrus squeezed his eyes shut and frowned in exasperation. "I woke up this morning to a village absolutely buzzing with a rumor that you had gone screaming to the governor about mermaids and murders and Shaman Orith! What the *blazes* did you think you were doing?"

The big man tried to keep his voice from booming clear out into the street. He was only partly successful.

"Now everyone is talking about you and your mother—"

"And you're worried you'll get swept up in rumors?" Emerson added. He realized a second too late he shouldn't have said it.

Cyrus came at him, and Emerson reflexively put his hands up. But the burly sailor just pushed him to the door. "You won't sass me in my own house, lad!"

He ejected Emerson back into the street and slammed the door.

If anyone hadn't been watching him before, they certainly were now. No longer worried about appearances, he ran to the village market.

He needed to get out of here, away from the disapproving stares. But first—he had to get some food.

"Four loaves of bread, please," he said, not meeting the baker's eyes. He slapped down the needed coins and hurried to the next stall.

"Cheese and jerky, please. However much this will buy." He laid down a few more coins and then turned away while the man got the items.

"You're the lad they're saying has finally gone pure bonkers! You believe mermaids talk!" the man said, sounding amused.

Emerson didn't even look toward him. He swallowed the bile that was rising in his throat and waited in silence.

The man frowned and handed him the wrapped food. Emerson left the booth without a word.

"That *was* the lad, wasn't it?" he heard the merchant say.

Someone answered him, "Yeah, no missing him. Pale as a *ghost* himself. Maybe if his mother had made him do honest work instead of all that reading and tinkering he'd not have lost it." Several people chuckled.

Despite his legs being tired, Emerson ran. Fueled by anger at the villagers, at Saria—for who else knew about his trip to Primus?—and anger at Shaman Orith for his heinous crimes. Part of his anger was more nebulous: his peaceful, invisible life had been all but destroyed.

He ran all the way out of town and down to the fence along the shore. He scaled it quickly, beyond caring who might see him, and tore down the beach. He rounded the base of the cliff, his boots splashing in the waves pushing up the sand.

After a short distance, he stopped and turned toward the cliff. A small cave entrance split the rock face like a mouth opening to receive the seawater. He ducked inside.

He paused for a moment to let his eyes adjust to the darkness. He could almost imagine he was five again, and his father's hands were covering his eyes. The cave was a secret his father had teased for nearly a whole week before finally taking a young Emerson to see it.

He had been thrilled and had begged his mother for years after to let him return. She hadn't liked how close it was to the waves, nor how they came right up into the cave and filled it halfway when the tide was in. Her answer had always been 'no,' especially after they lost his father to the sea.

His eyes now adjusted, Emerson looked around. The space was much smaller than in his childhood memory, but it would do.

A wide ledge ran across the back of the cave. Emerson pulled himself up onto it, knowing he would be dry even at high tide.

He set his bundles of food beside him and leaned his head against the rock wall at his back. The villagers' voices seemed to echo around the small chamber and he moaned, clapping a hand over his ears to drown them out.

His coat felt over-warm after running, but he was too tired to take it off. Emerson felt his eyes closing. The ebb and flow of the waves pulsed in his ears as he dropped into a heavy, dreamless sleep.

WORRY

Emerson drew his coat around him and stepped from the cave into the sea breeze. Stars twinkled overhead and the moon was just rising.

He shuffled through the damp sand, making his way quietly down the beach. Rounding the side of the cliff, he paused to see if anyone was about before scaling the fence.

Lights shone out from the village, but nobody was down by the shore after dark, especially not during the Hunting Time. Satisfied, Emerson crossed the fence and jogged toward the Kadwell cottage.

Light spilled from the windows. Keeping to the shadows as best he could, Emerson crept to the door.

Turning the handle, he opened it and slipped inside in one smooth motion.

"Emerson!" His mother jumped to her feet and ran to him. He registered her red, puffy eyes just before her face was buried in his chest. She hugged him so fiercely he could barely breathe.

"Mum," he grunted. She loosened her grip and leaned back to look at him. "I—I'm sorry, Mum. I know you've probably been worrying..."

"Worrying! Why, Emrie—I've been near crazy. Cyrus dropped by and said you had arrived in Chadwick early this morning! I told him you hadn't returned home yet and he told me what the villagers were saying."

Emerson hung his head. He hadn't been thinking clearly when leaving the village. He had only known he must get away from everyone until things died down. Once the governors brought Shaman Orith to justice, the village would see he wasn't crazy. Letting his mother know where he was had never even crossed his mind.

What is wrong with me?

"Where have you been, Emrie?"

"I went to the cave in the cliff, Mum. And—I'm sorry I didn't stop in to let you know. I felt like I was running for my life." Emerson shook his head sharply, irritated with himself. "I mean, I know I *wasn't* running for my life, but my whole body and my mind felt like I was. It's a stupid, stupid reaction. I'm so sorry, Mum."

Concern wrinkled around her eyes and she sighed. "Oh, son." She leaned her forehead against his shoulder, and then pulled him to sit at the kitchen table. "What's going on?" she asked wearily.

Emerson started at the beginning and told his mother about speaking with the governor. "He started out bored and then began mocking me. I went ahead with my story, though." His mother looked pleased that he had not given up.

"After I explained the whole situation and asked him to bring it to the governor of Stron Cay, he called me a half-wit, and when I tried to speak one more time, he—he questioned having installed you as schoolteacher for Chadwick."

Idina's eyes sparked with anger. "He called you a half-wit? He's lucky I don't send him my resignation of my own accord! Working for a man who insults my son!"

Emerson blinked. His mother was more concerned about the insult to him than the threat to her job. *She's incredible.*

"Mum, this part does have a good ending, though. Because when Saria and I were walking out of Primus, we almost knocked into—"

"Saria?" his mother interrupted, her eyebrows shooting upward. "Wait, back up... how did Saria end up in this story?"

Emerson explained bumping into Saria and her insisting on walking with him out of the town so they could talk. "Anyway, we almost bumped into this farmer who was staring at the semaphore tower. It was signaling Stron Cay, so whatever the governor said to my face, he must have later decided it was important enough to send a message."

His mother smiled. "You did good, son."

He returned her smile and then his face darkened. "But now I can't show my face in my own village without people talking like I'm truly a half-wit and a fool for bothering the governor."

"Before you'd spoken to a mermaid yourself, wouldn't you have believed their story to be a fairy tale?" his mother pointed out gently.

"Probably," Emerson had to admit. "But I wouldn't have insulted or teased the person telling the story."

"No, you wouldn't have," his mother agreed. "You're not that kind of person. And besides, I would have given you quite the lecture if you did."

Emerson snorted. "I believe that whole-heartedly. I think that might have something to do with why I'm not that kind of person!"

His mother chuckled.

"Well, it sounds like the whole matter is in the hands of the authorities now, son. You don't have to worry about it anymore," she said.

Emerson pursed his lips. "I'd still like to lay low until my story is proven, Mum. I don't particularly want to deal with the villagers staring at me like *I'm* the ghost."

His mother nodded. "Yes, we'll both stay out of the village for a bit," she agreed. "But you can sleep in your own bed."

"I'd better retrieve my things from the cave," Emerson said, jumping up and heading into his workshop for his communication invention. "And see if I can speak with Lilyse."

BETRAYAL

Emerson slipped away from his mother's cottage, his communication invention in a knapsack on his back. He climbed the fence and walked down to the water.

No sign of Lilyse.

He walked the length of the beach, checking the water for her blue glow, but saw nothing. Frowning, he crossed back over the fence and took the path leading to the top of the cliff.

Maybe they've already brought the Shaman to justice and she and the others are gone for good?

Scrambling to the top, he hurried forward and looked down at the sea. Several mermaids glowed a little further from the shore, where they normally were during the so-called Hunting Time.

He couldn't see them well enough to say whether one was Lilyse. "Where are you?" he murmured.

Since he had first felt her watching him several days ago, she had never been far from the shore.

Had she deserted him? Was it all a cruel joke on the part of the mermaids to stir up trouble for him?

NO! She saved my life twice. I believe her.

He refused to jump to the worst conclusion. There had to be a reason she wasn't nearby. But he knew he didn't want to miss her when she reappeared. He'd have to stay in the cave.

His mother would be disappointed. He trudged down the path, being careful of his footing in the dark, and back again to the cottage.

His mother looked up from her knitting. "How is she?"

Emerson pressed his lips and shook his head. "Couldn't find her."

His mother laid down her needles and looked thoughtful. "What will you do now?"

"I think I'd better stay in the cave so I won't miss her when she returns. And so things can die down in people's minds before I'm seen again."

His mother nodded slowly. With a sigh she said, "All right. If you're sure you'll be safe."

Emerson assured her he would take care of himself. She stuffed his knapsack with flasks of fresh water, additional food, and bedding. "If you can keep it dry, you can take a book, too," she offered.

"Oh!" Emerson said. "I would like that. Do you have anything with information on the semaphore language?"

Idina squinted thoughtfully and went to the book-lined wall. "Try this one." She tucked it into the top of his pack. Giving him a small smile, she brushed his unruly hair back from his face. "Check in after a day or two?"

"Of course, Mum." Emerson bent and gave her a quick, tight hug.

Two nights later, Emerson was wrapped in his quilt, studying semaphore by lantern-light on the cave ledge. The tide was in, and the water level came up to just a couple inches below him.

Something shifted in the corner of his eye, and Emerson looked up. A pale blue glow showed in the water just outside the cave's entrance. Fumbling with his knapsack. Emerson retrieved his communication invention—he decided he'd name the thing if it actually worked—and placed the flared end into the water.

"I'm in the cave," he spoke into the tube.

The glow grew brighter and Lilyse swam into the water filling the lower half of his cave.

"Hello! Can you hear me?" he asked.

She nodded, looking surprised to see he wasn't physically touching the water.

Now to test the other function.

He put the end of the tube to his ear and gestured to her.

"What is that? Did you make it?" Her voice came through, sounding a little muffled and quiet, but coming through nonetheless.

IT WORKS!

Emerson answered. "I don't have a good name for it yet, but it's my invention, yes. It's so I can speak to you and hear you without getting wet!"

"You're smart," she said.

Emerson felt his face heat, so he hurried to speak. "I went to the governor of Azul, Lilyse, and while I didn't think he had taken me seriously, it's going to work out after all. I saw his semaphore tower signaling Stron Cay after I'd left. He decided to send a message about your situation after all!" Emerson told her excitedly.

"Oh, Emerson! Thank you for taking up our plight! But—" her pale, semi-translucent face looked up at him. "Emerson, I'm worried."

"You were away for a few days. Is everything all right?"

"No," she said, looking down. "I got word from some of the others that a boat launched from Shaman Orith's village. It wasn't the ritual boat, though, which is very strange. As on your island, all other boats sit at their moorings this time of year. Only the Shaman's ritual boat goes out with the year's sacrifice, protected by some of his dark magic from our sabotage attempts. We can't get near it."

"Do you know where the boat was headed?"

Lilyse nodded. "Here. Well—to Azul, and I think to the port at Primus. I followed it the best I could, but, like the ritual boat, it is protected by the Shaman's magic."

Emerson bit his lip. "So what does this mean?"

"I think it's piloted by some of the Shaman's men. He must have seen the message your governor sent to Governor Milus."

Emerson felt a sort of shock fill his body. "No, I—I don't think that's what happened." He tapped his mother's book. "Semaphore messages about official business between the islands are sent in code. The Shaman couldn't have just intercepted a message going to Stron Cay's governor. The message must have been *for him*. Governor Aldan tipped him off."

He massaged his forehead. "The governor of Stron Cay still doesn't know you need justice."

Lilyse looked stricken. "And you are likely in grave danger, Emerson."

C⊙AT

Lilyse seemed certain that the Shaman's men were here to silence him. She said it was the way the man operated.

Emerson found it hard to believe a leader as well-followed as he could literally get away with murder without anyone standing up to him. They had argued about it for the better part of an hour. Lilyse finally made her point.

She said that was just it: he was so revered, nobody among his own followers would ever open their eyes to what he was doing and call it out for what it was. And if anyone did, they would likely find a young relative of theirs "selected" as the next sacrifice.

Eventually, the water level receded enough Lilyse had to bid him farewell until the next high tide. She swam back out to deeper water.

When low tide arrived, Emerson donned his coat against the wind he could hear howling outside. It had to be long past midnight now, but he still didn't feel like he could sleep a wink.

Is my life really in danger?

With his lantern shaded, he rounded the cliff, crossed the fence, and started up the path. The wind was biting and flecked with icy-cold droplets of rain. There were no stars tonight. Storm clouds made the sky an inky black.

Emerson slowly picked his way along the path. Without the moon and stars to go by, he wasn't sure of the exact time, but no lights shone from the Kadwell cottage or from the village, so he assumed it was quite a while yet until dawn.

When he finally arrived at the top of the path, the full force of the wind pushed against him, sending him staggering a few steps back.

Maybe coming up here tonight was a mistake, he thought, clutching his woolen coat more tightly about him. After the mild, spring weather they'd had recently, he had nearly forgotten the ferocity of the wind leading up to a good storm.

Not wanting to risk stumbling while up so high, he un-shuttered the lantern.

Again he stepped backward—but with more of a jump this time—and his heart began an uncomfortable hammering in his chest.

A small body lay on the cliff top a few yards from him.

The wind lifted caramel-colored curls, snapping them around as if in ghoulish greeting. "Saria?" Emerson gulped. *What the blazes! Was she—?*

He ran forward and touched the side of her soft neck lightly. She was barely warm, but she had a strong pulse. She stirred and whimpered—dreaming.

She's sleeping. But why on the cliff? In a storm!

Saria's small form was curled into a tight ball as she tried to make the best of the little warmth her coat had been providing. The fact that she was going to freeze to death in the winds of an impending storm hadn't registered with her brain enough to waken her.

Remembering the coolness of her skin, Emerson quickly stripped off his own coat and tucked its warmth around her. If he had felt the wind before, it was nothing compared to now. Gooseflesh prickled across every inch of his skin.

Why was he doing this for the girl who'd caused him nothing but grief?

Saria got home hours before me that day! She was the one who told everyone!

The remembrance of her betrayal blazed through his mind like a searing crack of lightning.

He grimaced at the sight of her snuggled into his coat while he bore the brunt of the cold wind in a thin shirt. For a moment he resented being such a decent human. Deep down, he knew he would never be able to leave her out in the elements.

He had to get her home.

"Saria!" he shook her. She groaned and stirred. Shaking her harder, he raised his voice over the wind whistling around the cliff. "Saria! Wake up; you need to go home before the storm hits."

She opened her eyes and stared at him for a moment, her face pale in the lantern-light, before recognition dawned. "Emerson! Oh, thank Omega!" She sat up and threw her arms around him in a startling embrace.

Surprised, Emerson pushed her off and said gruffly, "Time to go home, Saria."

"Where's your coat? Oh." She stood and tried to shrug it off, but he pushed it back onto her shoulders.

"Keep it for now. Come on."

"Emerson, where have you been? Are you okay?" she asked, her voice annoyingly reedy against the noise of the wind and the waves below.

Without replying, Emerson picked up the lantern and guided her to the path. The wind was still gusting, and it pushed Saria even harder than it had him. She knocked into him and breathlessly apologized.

Switch places with her. Shield her from the worst of the wind, his conscience said. He tamped down the thought and continued stoically forward. He was already doing enough for her.

It was slow going because the wind seemed bent on tangling Saria in her own skirts. After she'd had to spin in circles for the fourth time to unwind the bulk of fabric from around her legs, Emerson grew impatient.

Hoping she wouldn't smack him, he picked her up, cradling her in both coats, and jogged the rest of the way down the steep path. Holding her helped him to warm up a bit, not that he cared to admit it.

A lock of her loose hair blew across his face. It smelled like warm vanilla.

He shook it away, annoyed.

At the base of the path, he unceremoniously plopped her down on her own feet.

"Thank you," she said, barely loud enough to be heard over the storm closing in.

Emerson shrugged silently and jerked his head toward the village.

Just then, the clouds opened up with fury.

CONFESSION

Emerson pulled Saria under an outcropping of rock to his right. The deluge had already nearly soaked him through in the first few seconds.

She's probably fine wearing two coats and all.

There was very little space under the rock, and he grimaced at the fact that they had to huddle so close. He angled away from her. There was nothing he'd rather do less than be trapped in a small space with this obnoxious girl who caused him trouble at every turn.

Why, she was causing him trouble right now! He tried, but couldn't stop a cold shiver.

"Emrie—" she said. The wind tried its hardest to drown out her voice.

"Don't call me that," he said sharply. "That's my mother's nickname for me, and you certainly don't get to use it."

"I'm sorry, Emerson. But listen—"

Emerson cut her off. "I know what you did—I know you told everyone I'd been to see the governor.

And I want you to stay away from me, Saria. I mean it. I'll walk you back to your house and then that's the last I want to see of you. I've let you walk into my life and mess it up enough. No more." He tamped down the tendril of guilt that wormed its way into his heart. Sometimes being firm with someone came across as mean. It couldn't really be helped.

She was silent a moment, but rumbling thunder filled the void.

Emerson stole a glance at her face, dimly lit by his lantern. Tears tracked down her cheeks and she was biting her lip. *Great. She's going to make me feel bad with tears now.*

With a sudden movement, she pulled his coat off her shoulders and threw it into his lap. "Emerson Kadwell, why do you always cut me off before I can say what I want to say?" she challenged, anger flashing in her eyes. "You assume instead of listening. All the things I try to say never get spoken because you just shut me down."

She hunched into her own coat, the way she had the morning she found him on the cliff. Right before she went and told the village he had wanted to jump. He narrowed his eyes. What was she even talking about?

"So this time, it's my turn. You be quiet and listen." She took a shaky breath, seeming to steady her anger into something that propelled her. "I teased you when we were little. Believe what you might, it was only so I could get you to pay attention to me. You were so shy, but when I teased, you actually talked to me.

"Silly, yes. It was the foolish reasoning of a child. But, Emerson, I've grown up."

Emerson picked up the coat she'd thrown at him and put it on. The inside was warm.

"Have you?" he asked.

"Hush," she said forcefully. "I don't speak to you to mock you. I don't visit you to annoy you. I like you, Emerson. I like you *because* you're different. You use your mind. You think—except for when it comes to me. You're even nice—to people who aren't me.

"You accuse me of creating a rumor the morning I found you up on the cliff, yet you have *no* proof I did that. Can't you think of any other way people might have started talking?" Her gaze bored into him for a moment. He wasn't sure whether he was supposed to speak now or not so he shrugged and looked away.

In reality, his mind was racing, going over the events of the day in question. He realized it was possible he had jumped to a conclusion.

"Emerson, I *hiked* up that stupidly rocky trail to warn you it was light enough to see you up there. Because I know you don't like being noticed. Because I know you tend to get teased. Because I *cared*." She lowered her eyes and waited for a loud rumble of thunder to pass.

"And by the time you'd brushed me off and I'd gotten back to the village, someone else had seen you up there. I passed a couple sailors speculating. They knew before I got back. *Before, Emerson!*"

She was trembling now, but he didn't know whether from cold or from anger.

"And in your workshop, I was starting to say that people only tease you because you're different, BUT— and you cut me off before I got this far—at least one person in this village *likes* you because of those differences. Me."

Before Emerson could react, she was barreling on, raising her voice over the wind and pounding rain.

"You think I told everyone you had visited the governor with some tale about the mermaids and Shaman Orith? Well, think back for just a moment and try to remember what you actually told me, what I *actually knew* when I left Primus."

With a feeling of surprise, Emerson realized she only knew he had spoken with Governor Aldan.

"I didn't know any of those details. That means someone else has sabotaged your life this time, Emerson. Not me. And do you know what? I have spent years now trying to be your friend, and I don't think I deserve this kind of treatment from you.

"I would have hoped by now you'd be willing to give me the benefit of the doubt. But you've never allowed yourself to see what's really going on."

She scrubbed the tears from her reddened cheeks and then spoke quietly. He could barely hear her over the storm. "Goodbye, Emerson."

Before he could say anything, she had left the protection of the rocky outcropping and was running toward her home through the pouring rain.

ALONE

Emerson stepped dismally into his mother's cottage. Shedding his coat, he stepped to the fire his mother had just lit.

Frowning, she said, "Emerson, it's not even dawn! What's happened? You're soaked through! Have you been in the sea again?"

He shook his head. Listening to the storm moaning around the cottage, he commented, "The weather is so fitful this time of year. Balmy one minute and furious the next."

Idina shook her head. "You're avoiding my question, Emrie."

He winced. Saria had tried to call him that: the name his mother used when showing her fondness for him. He was such a fool.

Such an utter, complete, useless fool.

His mother had left her chair by the fire and returned with a stack of dry clothes. "Change," she ordered, "and then come sit."

115

Obeying, Emerson returned a short time later and sat cross-legged before the fireplace.

"Now," his mother said firmly, "tell me what's happened."

"Not much," Emerson said, laughing bitterly, "I've just discovered that the Shaman sent some men here to Azul, that the governor probably tipped him off, and that I've lost a friend I didn't even know I had. And that was due to my own foolish pride." He trailed off into muttering.

His mother stared at him, looking confused. "Start with that last one and work backward," she said.

With a sigh, Emerson said, "Mum, have you ever misjudged someone so completely that no matter what they do or say you'll always see it as a bad thing?"

His mother's face softened in the firelight and a knowing look played across her features. "Is this about Saria?"

He gaped.

"Don't be so surprised, son. The girl has always looked on you kindly. You've seemed oblivious or offended by her interest. You said she spread rumors about you on the cliff... is that what this is about?"

Emerson pinched the bridge of his nose and grimaced. "Mum, I made such a huge mistake—she didn't spread those rumors. I thought she did, but—but—I just jumped to the first thought that came to my mind. I believed the worst possibility immediately. Blazes! I gave a *mermaid* the benefit of the doubt and jumped straight to accusations with Saria. Over and over," he said brokenly.

"So she didn't spread the rumors?" his mother asked quietly.

He shook his head. "No. Someone else saw me up there, because, as she warned me, it was getting light enough."

"Oh, son." His mother's voice held a painful note of reproach.

"And I've done it over and over, Mum! I've cut her off before she can even speak enough for me to know—*anything* true about her!"

"You don't know the real Saria," his mother said. "Just the version your assumptions have constructed."

"Yes," Emerson whispered. *That's disgusting. People do that to me all the time.*

"Like we've always done with the mermaids," his mother mused.

Emerson groaned and buried his face in his hands.

"Emrie," his mother said, "there's good news in all this. I know a young man who threw away some long-held assumptions to find out the truth about mermaids for himself. Who took a risk and learned how to *hear* them."

Emerson looked up slowly. His mother's words lit a small, hopeful fire inside him. Maybe, just maybe there was a way to make things right with Saria.

He wasn't sure anything he could say or do would ever be enough to atone for how unjustly he'd treated her, but all he could do was try.

"I have to go see her tomorrow," he said quietly.

They were silent together for a few minutes before his mother said, "What is this about the Shaman and Governor Aldan?"

Emerson rubbed a hand over his face wearily. "I finally spoke with Lilyse tonight—last night, whatever it is now—and I told her I thought Governor Aldan had sent a message to Governor Milus after all. Unfortunately, it looks like that's probably not the case."

"He sent a message to Shaman Orith instead, didn't he," his mother said, piecing things together herself.

"That's what we think based off the fact that a boat left the Shaman's village for Primus. Lilyse thinks I could be in some danger."

Idina's gaze snapped from the crackling fire to Emerson's face. "What kind of danger?" she asked.

"I don't know for sure, Mum." He yawned.

"I think you ought to sleep in a real bed for a few hours," his mother said gently.

Although he wanted to put up a fight and tell her he should stay in the cave in case Lilyse needed something, he allowed her to push him toward his bedroom.

APOLOGY

Emerson had been so intent on his goal, he hadn't really noticed the stares. He had purposefully woven through the streets of the village until he stood at the Beggleys' front door.

Hesitating just a moment, he removed his cap and knocked.

After a moment in which he barely breathed, someone came to the door. He hoped Saria wouldn't turn him away as soon as she saw him on the stoop.

Instead of Saria, Madge, the housekeeper answered. "Yes?"

"Um..." Emerson's opening words had been planned for Saria. He couldn't very well say, "I'm truly sorry for upsetting you the other night. I've been doing a lot of thinking... can we talk?" to the housekeeper.

Madge raised a grey eyebrow, waiting.

"I'm—I'm sorry. I was hoping to speak with Saria..."

The woman looked him up and down for a moment. "I will allow it, but only briefly. She's finally awake." Emerson was confused by her answer, but he hurried to step through the open door before she changed her mind.

The housekeeper led him to a bedroom steeped in dreariness with the curtains drawn. "Speak quietly. I'll show you out in no more than 3 minutes." She hovered just outside the doorway.

Realization dawned on Emerson as he entered the darkened room. Saria was tucked up in her bed under a mound of quilts. Her caramel-colored hair fanned out on the white pillow. Her face was flushed and her eyes were closed.

He approached and stood staring awkwardly, consumed with guilt. *She's sick!* She had run off into a cold rain because of him. *Blazes!* She had been out at night in the first place because she had been looking for him—worrying about him.

Saria's eyes slid open and took a moment to focus on his face. Her eyebrows puckered.

"I'm so sorry," he murmured, kneeling beside the bed and impulsively taking her over-warm hand. "Will you be all right?"

She withdrew her hand and said, "Madge says if I rest quietly I'll be right as rain in a few days. I'm not so sure about that expression." Her voice was hoarse and breathy—tired.

His planned words forgotten, Emerson blurted, "I've been horrible to you, and—I'm so sorry. I didn't see the real you. I didn't really *hear* you, and I was inexcusably rude. I'm... sorry." He ran a hand through his hair frustratedly. "Sorry is not enough, I know."

Saria was silent for a moment. "I am sorry I teased you when we were little," she said quietly.

"No—no, don't apologize," Emerson pleaded, covering his face with his hands. "Just—just listen? If you feel well enough to, that is. I want to show you how sorry I am by telling you something I've told very few people."

"Is it about the mermaids?" Saria asked, her dull eyes sparkling a little now.

"Yes, it's about the mermaids," Emerson said.

Saria's eyes slid to the doorway. "Madge," she said, raising her voice just a bit above the whisper she had been using. The housekeeper appeared instantly, a question on her face. "I knew you were there. Leave Emerson and me to talk?" she asked.

"It's highly improper, my dear—" the woman began.

"Please, Madge? I'm still able to scream, I'm sure," she said, slight amusement showing in her eyes.

The housekeeper humphed but did as Saria asked.

She's still thinking of me, Emerson realized with a shock. *She knows having someone listening in would make me uncomfortable.*

"Thank you for trusting me," he said.

"I trust that you're not going to be improper in any way," she said, eyeing him. "But beyond that—" She fell silent, an undecided pucker appearing between her brows again.

Her words stung, but Emerson knew he deserved it.

He pulled a nearby chair closer to her bedside and sat. "Well," he said, pondering his hands, "the rumors are partly right. I did go speak to the governor about mermaids and murder and Shaman Orith. What they don't include is that I got the story of the murders from a mermaid who asked me to seek justice for them."

Saria listened with wide eyes as he told her the story of meeting Lilyse, of her saving his life twice, and of her request to bring Shaman Orith to justice.

"Oh, Emerson, that's terrible!" she exclaimed softly when he'd explained about the Sea Appeasement sacrifices. "How does he get away with it?"

"Probably a combination of people not knowing—we certainly haven't heard about it here on Azul—and those who do know refusing to see the truth of the situation," Emerson said sorrowfully.

It felt good to share his story with her. She was an attentive listener, but he could see she was beginning to wilt.

"I should probably go," he said finally. "You're looking very tired, and I could never forgive myself if I caused a relapse. Thank you for listening."

"Thank you for trusting me enough to tell me. You really don't believe I started the rumors?"

"I wouldn't have told you all that if I did," Emerson said, rising.

He lingered awkwardly. "When you're well, if you want to stop by the workshop at any time, you'll be welcome from here on out. I promise to learn to listen. I hope I can make it up to you somehow. I hope you can forgive me."

She didn't say anything, but regarded him thoughtfully with a tiny, sad smile.

Maybe, just maybe she will trust me again someday.

He was surprised by how much he hoped so.

SHADOWS

Emerson paused a moment on the stoop after the Beggleys' door clicked shut behind him. He was glad he had come. He sincerely hoped Saria would want to attempt a friendship again. He would make sure the effort wasn't one-sided this time.

He shook his head. "I still can't believe I only saw annoyances when she was really just being friendly," he muttered. A man passing by looked at him strangely.

Okay, so talking to myself probably isn't what my reputation needs right now. I should get out of here.

He still felt keeping his distance from the gossip in the village was a good course of action, but some things were more important. Such as patching up his relationship with the friend he hadn't known he had.

Keeping his head down, he walked quickly down the street. His scalp prickled and he felt as if he was being watched. Rubbing the back of his neck, he told himself to ignore it. Practically the whole village was noticing him these days.

Deciding to take a less-busy route out of the village, Emerson turned down a narrow, empty side street.

He rubbed the back of his neck again. Why hadn't the feeling of being watched gone away?

He glanced behind him.

Two men had followed him into the alley. *How long have they been tailing me?*

He paused and turned, hoping to discern their intent. One was a stocky Cayan, and the other was a scarred red-headed man with a large mustache. Both had long hair braided into many small braids—the preferred style of Shaman Orith's devout followers—but interwoven into their braids were multi-colored ribbons and glinting charms.

Something in his gut told him these were no ordinary followers of Shaman Orith.

They had to be the men from the boat Lilyse had spotted. And they were here. In Chadwick. Following him.

The glint of a knife propelled Emerson into action. He spun and took off running in the opposite direction. Thankful he knew the streets and alleys of Chadwick well, he turned sharply to the right and kept running. He could hear the men following, and he hazarded a glance behind him.

For the moment, he was staying ahead of them, but he knew he didn't have much stamina when it came to long distances. He needed to be smart.

He passed another street and then abruptly turned right again. The market was just ahead. If he could make it that far, he would at least be in a public place. They hadn't made any move to attack or chase him while he was on a busier street, so he hoped to lose them.

Something prompted him to glance back again— just in time to see the scar-faced man throw the knife.

Emerson flinched left and the knife just missed him, clattering to the hard earth a pace ahead of him. Barely thinking, he slowed just enough to scoop it up on his way by. He certainly didn't want them picking it up and throwing it again.

When he popped out into the market, he dodged quickly between several stalls and plunged forward into the thickest part of the crowd.

Ducking down behind a booth, he peered back toward the side street. His pursuers exited and slowed to a casual walk, but they looked all around them alertly. Emerson moved through the market as quickly as he could. He stayed in a crouch and behind booths for cover.

Finally reaching the opposite edge of the market, he stood and darted down another street. Glancing behind him, he saw the Shaman's men scanning the faces of the crowd.

He ran harder.

A commotion arose. They must have seen him. He skidded and headed left along a row of houses.

A memory welled up inside him: a memory of some boys teasing him when he was younger. They'd chased him from the market, and he had shimmied through a broken fence slat into a yard with a large tree . He'd managed to make it up the tree and remain hidden by the leafy boughs while the boys wondered where he'd gone.

He hadn't known it at the time, but the tree was in Cyrus Hammer's yard.

Emerson didn't particularly want to have anything to do with Cyrus or his tree, but he didn't have time now to be picky. He vaulted over the low fence. Out of the corner of his eye, he saw a curtain move in the window of Cyrus' house.

By the time the men arrived at the spot, panting, he was well hidden by the tree above their heads.

They paused a moment to catch their breath, and then they split up. Knocking on the nearby doors, they asked if anyone had seen a lad of his description. Thankfully, none of the neighbors had noticed anything.

When they knocked on Cyrus' door, Emerson held his breath. He was pretty sure the big man had seen him go up the tree.

INFORMATION

Emerson gripped the tree branch so hard his knuckles turned white. He clamped down on his nervousness and forced himself to take long, even breaths. Getting shaky right then would probably cause him to be discovered.

He couldn't afford to rustle the tree.

"No, I don't think so," Cyrus' loud voice boomed in response to the Shaman's men. They pressed him, and he growled in his usual manner, "I already told you I didn't see the lad. Are you calling my truthfulness into question? Now, get away from my place. I don't want to have to make you."

The Shaman's men scowled, but they did as he said. They must have had orders not to make too much of a scene. Cyrus banged his door shut. Emerson waited until they were out of sight before he loosened his grip on the branch he clung to.

Relief made him feel weak for a moment, and he almost jumped out of his skin when someone hissed his name.

"Emerson! Come down!"

Cyrus had opened his door just a crack and was calling him in the quietest voice Emerson had ever heard from the man.

He really did see me. I wonder why he covered for me like that...

Carefully, Emerson climbed down out of the tree and dropped onto the grass. Cyrus beckoned him urgently, his gaze roaming the street for any sign of the men.

Emerson hurried toward the house, and ducked inside as Cyrus opened the door wider. Unsure what to expect considering how things had gone the last time, he was silent a moment.

"Thank you for covering for me," he finally said.

Cyrus nodded gravely. "You seemed to be in a good heap of trouble. If I'm not mistaken, those men are high-ranking followers of Shaman Orith. They certainly weren't looking to invite you to tea, Emerson. You realize they might have orders to kill you?"

Emerson nodded, his hand going to his belt where he'd tucked the knife. "I think they do," he said, bringing it out.

Looking at it closely for the first time, Emerson was surprised. The blade gleamed as if it had just received a good polishing. The handle was intricately carved and stained a brilliant red. The carvings were inlaid with what he assumed to be gold.

He looked up at Cyrus whose mouth had dropped open.

"Lad, this ain't good at all," the big man sighed. "That's a very unique knife. I'd say the owner is a very influential man."

Cyrus frowned and then continued. "You'd best stay out of town. I did a little digging, looking for who spread the news that you'd spoken to the governor. It seems a stranger showed up in town the night before you returned and talked of nothing else while at Millie's Pub."

It was Emerson's turn to frown.

"There's more," Cyrus said. "One man told me as soon as the fellow had finished his drinks, he left town—headed north."

"Almost as if his only purpose in coming to Chadwick was to start the rumors?" Emerson narrowed his eyes. "There *was* a messenger who rode out of Primus as I was leaving."

"Aye, your friend the governor probably betrayed you twice, lad. Once to the Shaman and once to your village."

"It's a good way to keep people ignorant," Emerson laughed bitterly. "Make me out to be a fool *before* they've had a chance to hear the whole story."

There was a moment of awkward silence, and then Emerson said, "I guess you're right: I need to stay out of town for several reasons."

Cyrus was frowning. "I mean it, s—lad. Although we've had our differences and our battles, I don't want to see any harm come to you."

Emerson ducked his head. Today was the day for apologies. "I'm sorry about what I said before. Thank you for letting me know what you discovered. I'll be careful."

Cyrus let him stay until the sun began to set. Then, slipping through the shadows, Emerson made his way out of Chadwick and down toward the water. He stopped in at his mother's cottage and let her know some of what he and Cyrus had discussed.

He didn't tell her too much, though. He didn't think there was any sense in worrying her with all the details of his escapade.

Just letting her know the Shaman's men were about was enough for her. She agreed he should keep to his cave for at least the next several days.

DANGER

Emerson's eyes popped open. The dazzling sunlight outside the cave told him he had overslept.

After waiting up for the tide to come in and speaking with Lilyse, he had found it hard to fall asleep. Finally, just as the blackness was lightening to grey, he had dozed off.

What had awakened him now?

Waves pushed up the beach outside his cave, reaching the entrance, but not yet far enough to spill inside. Something was disturbing the rhythmic rushing sound.

Splash. Splash. Splash. Splash.

Someone was walking through the shallow waves. Emerson leapt from the ledge he'd been lying on and crossed the cave. He flattened himself against the wall to the right of the entrance. Hopefully he would be able to determine if the person was here to harm him before they noticed him there in the shadows.

After a few tense moments, a silhouette darkened the entrance. One he recognized easily.

"Emerson?" his mother's voice called nervously.

"Mum! You had me worried," he said, sagging in relief. "Come on in."

His mother shuffled into the dim cave, her eyes taking a moment to adjust to the dimness.

"Emrie—thank Omega you're safe!" She enfolded him in a tight hug.

"I can't believe you came out here, Mum!" Emerson said, looking down at her curiously. "You hate the water! Something has happened, hasn't it." He leaned back and took in her exhausted face and red-rimmed eyes. "What is it?"

"Cyrus came by early this morning. He told me something terrible happened last night. Someone found a lad in an alleyway. He was beat up and barely alive. Roughed up so badly—oh, Emerson." Idina covered her mouth with her hand and shook her head.

"Is he going to be okay?" Emerson asked. His mother nodded, but lacked conviction. "I don't understand why—"

"You're wondering why Cyrus came to me? The boy—he was tall and had dark hair..."

"Like me..." Emerson gasped, horror searing through his body as he realized the import of his mother's news. "Did you think it was me?"

"Thankfully, no. Cyrus knew who it was when he brought the news. But, Emerson, he says it was likely the Shaman's men who did it, and that *they* thought it was you. He says you might not realize just how much danger you're truly in."

"If I didn't before, I certainly do now," Emerson said darkly.

Isn't it sort of my fault this boy got beat up? They thought they'd caught me!

Bile rose in his throat, and he clenched his hands.

When would this be over? Nobody would be safe until something was done.

"Mum!" Emerson said, gripping her shoulder and peering at her seriously in the dim light. "If the Shaman's men are this serious about getting to me, you could be in danger the minute they figure out they got the wrong lad."

"I hadn't thought of that—"

"The governor knows exactly whose son I am, and if he's the one who tipped them off—" Emerson straightened. "Mum, promise me you'll go straight to Cyrus' house and stay there."

Idina raised an eyebrow and protested, "That wouldn't be proper, Emerson."

"Have someone else you trust come too, then."

"But... Mr. Hammer? I know the way you feel about him," his mother said pointedly.

Emerson sighed. "Mum, there are things about him that I find annoying. Less than ideal. But he really does care about what happens to you and even me. He will protect you, I know it."

Her eyebrows puckered as she tried to hold back tears. "I am so proud of you, Emrie."

Emerson gave her a quick hug. He stared at the floor of the cave and licked his lips nervously. How should he say this? "I—I'd like you to know I want you to be happy," he said. "And Mum, I won't decide for you what that means. If someday you think Cyrus is right for you..." He trailed off unsure how to phrase it.

"I would have your blessing?" his mother finished, giving him a watery smile.

"Yes, I suppose that's what I mean."

She squeezed his shoulder.

A bit of seawater sloshed into the cave and Idina reluctantly said she had to go before the tide came in any further. She pressed a new, blank notebook into her son's hand. He smiled gratefully.

She always knows just what I need.

Emerson made her promise once more to go straight to Cyrus' house. She agreed and told him to be extra careful.

"Don't worry, Mum," Emerson said. "I'm working up a plan. It will require me to go to Miren, so you probably won't hear from me for several days. Try not to worry."

With one last glance backward, his mother left the cave and picked her way through the sliding waves. Emerson was alone.

PLAN

Emerson spent the better part of the day scribbling and sketching in the new notebook his mother had brought him. At first he found it hard to concentrate. Worry for his mother's safety, for the health of the lad who had been attacked, and guilt over the trouble he had unintentionally brought to Chadwick distracted him.

Eventually, though, in the quietness of the cave, his focus returned and he became completely engrossed in his planning.

When he was satisfied with the sketches, Emerson tucked the notebook away in his knapsack and ate a little food. He then stretched out on the padding of his wool coat. For safety, his plan would need to be carried out after night had fallen, so now was his chance to rest.

He leaned back and focused on the waves sloshing in and out of the cave. Eventually he slept.

His dreams were a weird mixture of running through the streets of Primus and Chadwick and painting wooden boards with pitch.

The nightmare didn't make an appearance.

When Emerson woke, the floor of his cave was dry except for the few places where water always remained in puddles. The light outside was just changing from golden to a dusky blue. The sun was nearly set.

Emerson's stomach grumbled and he ate some cheese and bread, watching as the world outside slipped further and further into the darkness of night. Stars appeared. He realized with a bit of surprise that there would be no moon that night.

That's probably for the best. Less chance of being seen by someone. Less chance of being attacked.

When he was sure it was time, he took his knapsack and the unlit lantern, left the cave, and quietly padded along the beach. Rounding the cliff, he stayed in the shadows long enough to be sure nobody was about. He quickly climbed the fence and jogged toward the Kadwell cottage.

No light shone through the windows since his mother had long since left for Cyrus' house as he'd made her promise. Emerson again waited in a deep shadow. There could be someone watching the place.

All was still.

Trying to minimize the groan of the hinges, Emerson opened the door of the rough lean-to attached to the side of the cottage. He couldn't see much in the darkness, so he felt with his fingers. The hinges were attached with screws.

He ran his hands lightly over the whole door, wincing as he picked up a splinter. It seemed solid. There were a few narrow gaps between the boards, but he could easily fill them.

Silently, he entered the cottage. Feeling his way in the darkness rather than lighting any lamps, he made his way into the workshop. After covering the window, he lit his lantern.

His tools and invention models cast long, flickering shadows in the lantern light. Everything had a fine layer of dust on it.

Resisting the urge to give things a good wiping, Emerson brought out his notebook and opened it to one of the lists he'd made. Working quickly, he packed tools he would need into his knapsack. Snatching a particular screwdriver, he stuck it in his belt.

Hoisting the knapsack onto his back, he tucked the only thing too large for it—the small keg of pitch—under his arm. Extinguishing his lantern he crept carefully back out of the cottage.

Working only by feel, Emerson unscrewed the hinges holding the lean-to door in place. It was challenging to do by himself and in the dark, but after a good while, the thing was free.

Carrying everything was challenging, too, but by hooking the lantern to his knapsack and partially dragging the door, he made it to the fence. The door would be too hard to carry over with him, so he threaded it between two of the slats.

He winced every time the door scraped more noisily against the fence.

It's probably not half as loud as it seems, he told himself. Still, he breathed a sigh of relief when he'd pushed it all the way through to the other side.

Quickly scaling the fence himself and dropping over onto the sand, he hurried everything back to the cave, glad that the incoming tide would smooth out his tracks and the weird trail made by dragging the door.

When he reached the cave, he set to work by lantern light.

The door was rustically built of rough boards. As he had already known, there were narrow gaps between these boards, but with the supplies he had brought back from the workshop, he would be able to patch them.

As he worked, the waves began to spill into the cave. By the time the bottom half of the cave had filled with sea water, the door was solid. Emerson glanced up and smiled as Lilyse's blue glow appeared under the water in the entrance.

He retrieved his speaking tube, as he was now calling it, and greeted her. "Hello, Lilyse. I have a lot to tell you."

She smiled but looked concerned. "Good news, I hope?"

Emerson bit his lip. "I'm afraid it's mostly bad news, actually. But there's hope at least..." He filled her in on everything that had happened since the last time they spoke. The governor's double betrayal, that the

Shaman's men were in Chadwick, and the beating of the lad who resembled him.

Lilyse shivered. "Didn't I tell you this was how the Shaman works?"

Emerson nodded, lost in thought.

"There's something else you're not telling me," Lilyse's muffled voice said.

"What? Oh, it's nothing." Emerson shook his head.

The mermaid laughed musically. "Then why did your face turn red and almost ashamed-looking?"

"It's personal," Emerson said, sheepishly rubbing the back of his neck.

"And I'm a ghost who's bound to the water. Who would I tell?"

"The other mermaids? And you'll all have a good laugh?"

Lilyse sighed and spoke as if he were a little child. "Emerson, do you really think I'm like that?"

"No," he admitted. "You're not at all." He told her about Saria.

Her glowing, semi-transparent face looked remarkably wistful when he was done. "Try hard, Emerson," she said softly. "Win her back. You can't underestimate the power of true friends at a time like this."

Emerson nodded and then reached for the patched door lying next to him on the ledge. "After I paint the underside of this with pitch, it will be a raft."

"And what's that for?" Lilyse asked, looking puzzled.

"I have an invention in mind that just might still get you all justice. But to assemble it, and avoid being killed by the Shaman's men, I need to leave the island. Tonight."

"You want to go to Miren to work on this invention," Lilyse guessed.

"Exactly," Emerson said. "It's so sparsely populated I'll be able to work in peace, and it's close enough I can shuttle supplies from my workshop at night. There's just one thing—"

"Yes?"

He looked down at the girl glowing in the water below him. "I need the mermaids' help propelling the raft between the islands."

VOYAGE

The pitch had made the cave smell terrible, and Emerson couldn't wait to leave. When he had tested that the improvised raft didn't leak, he loaded his meager bedding and food stores onto it. Getting on, he pushed against the cave wall with his hands and propelled it toward the entrance.

The tide was beginning to go out again by then, so Lilyse had said the mermaids would wait for him outside the cave.

Sure enough, she and five others floated just under the surface of the waves, waiting. It was the first time Emerson had met any of the others, and the tragedy of their situation struck him heavily as he looked around at their tired, but hopeful faces.

Using the speaking tube, he greeted them and explained the general plan. They all nodded in agreement, seeming a bit reluctant to speak.

"If you need to say anything, I can hear you with my invention," he told them.

One or two of them said a shy "hello" and "thank you."

"Are you the talkative one, Lilyse?" Emerson asked. She rolled her eyes and gave his raft a little shove.

"The water will be a bit choppy partway to Miren," she said. "There's a current. Be sure you're holding on."

Emerson nodded. Lilyse signaled to the others and took the rope handles Emerson had attached to the left and right sides of his raft. With the unnatural way they interacted with the water, the mermaids were able to swim very fast, bearing the raft between them.

This is a little unnerving. Not at all like being on a boat.

The lean-to door raft skimmed smoothly over the waves with none of the rocking of a boat. Emerson looked down into the water. The mermaids were perfectly visible in the moonless dark, their glowing brighter than he'd ever seen it.

Lilyse caught him staring and smiled. Then she pointed up ahead.

We must be coming up on that current.

He checked that everything was tied securely and then hunkered down, holding fast to the ropes.

A moment later, the raft bucked on a choppy wave and the mermaids on the left side lost their grip on the ropes. When it splashed back down into the water, they grabbed hold again. Lilyse seemed to be giving directions about how to keep the raft more stable.

Despite their best efforts, the ride was still bumpy for the next few minutes. Emerson clung to his ropes, trying hard not to think about the endless depth of the water beneath him, nor the powerful current that could whisk him away.

Surely Lilyse would be able to save him again if something happened.

Abruptly, the water calmed and he raised his head. Out of the water rose the black silhouette of Miren against the starlit sky.

He peered over the edge of the raft and met Lilyse's questioning gaze. He gave her a nod, assuring her he was none the worse for wear.

He shivered slightly as the sea breeze passed over his damp clothes. He would have to think of a way to stay dry the next time he crossed from one island to the next.

Something tapped the wood underneath him. Startled, he looked over the edge. Lilyse gestured to her ear, and he quickly put the speaking tube into the water.

"Danae, here, has spent time around Miren's coast. She knows of a sheltered and unpopulated area just ahead and to the west a bit," she told him.

Emerson glanced to the other mermaid, nodded, and said, "That sounds perfect."

The dark mass of land loomed larger and larger. As he looked over the edge of the raft, the mermaids' glowing began to illuminate sand beneath them as the floor of the sea sloped up to the beach. When there was no more room for the mermaids to fit between the bottom and the surface of the water, they stopped swimming and gave the raft a gentle push up the beach.

It ground to a halt, waves gently lapping around it on the untouched sand stretching along Miren's western coast.

Emerson got off the raft and pulled it further up the beach. Taking his speaking tube, he went back down to the water.

"Thank you for such a safe and quick voyage," he said. "I will unload what I have and set it back among the trees. Then, if you're willing, we should go back for more of the supplies I will need."

Lilyse looked briefly at the other mermaids. They agreed with solemn nods. She gave Emerson a smile. "Anything you need. You're the one helping us."

Emerson's heart swelled with the faith they put in him. He only hoped his untested invention and the accompanying plan worked.

It could very well be their last hope.

MIREN

Something tickled Emerson's nose and an unusual noise nudged him into unwilling consciousness. He blinked against the bright light filtering through his eyelids. Green treetops waved gently above him and birdsong—far more pleasant than the gulls he was used to ignoring—wrapped the woods in peacefulness.

He sat up and a small butterfly danced away.

He was on the island of Miren. Beneath him was the tarp that had kept him and his supplies dry on the trips between the two islands. He glanced around, eyeing the piles he'd unloaded rather haphazardly in the dark the night before. Getting his bearings the best he could, he surmised it was late morning. He blinked hard and scrubbed at his face.

Scrambling stiffly to his feet, he moved to the piles of supplies and tools, checking everything against the lists in his notebook.

It was all there. He could begin work.

Emerson perched on his keg of pitch and ate a quick breakfast of slightly stale bread and some water from his flask. When he was done, he wiped his mouth and took a moment to study his sketches.

He worked hard all day: smoothing and evening up boards, cutting them to several different lengths, and laying everything out in the order he'd need for assembly. By the time all the preparations were complete, it was growing too dark to see well.

Going down to the water for the first time that day, Emerson found Lilyse waiting for him. "Hello," he greeted, placing the speaking tube in the water.

"Hello," she said, "did you have a good day working?"

"Yes. It's going well. I only wish I could finish faster."

Lilyse nodded. "So far the Shaman's boat has not gone out for this year's sacrifice. It could be any day now."

"I assume you have someone keeping tabs on that?" Emerson asked.

"Yes—Danae has a couple of girls watching. Normally, she spends this time of year as close to the Shaman's village as possible. She tries, every year, to save the sacrifice even though the Shaman's magic keeps her away." Lilyse spoke quietly. "She was the first, you know."

Emerson's eyes widened. "Was she?"

"Yes, it's been 31 years for her."

Emerson couldn't fathom it. "Why is she here instead of near Stron Cay?" he asked.

Lilyse gestured to her left. "Why don't you ask her yourself? She's coming this way."

So far, Danae hadn't spoken to him at all. She seemed very quiet and aloof. But when she drew closer, he greeted her. "Good evening, Danae."

She gave him a small nod.

"Emerson was just telling me he made good progress on the invention today," Lilyse told her.

"Thank you," Danae said quietly.

"Lilyse said you try to stay near Stron Cay this time of year," Emerson said gently. "If you need to go, please don't feel like I'm keeping you here."

The mermaid smiled sadly. "I have some of the others keeping watch. If the Shaman prepares his ritual ship they will send word, and I will have time enough to get there."

Emerson nodded. Should he ask her more?

"I'm very fast at navigating these waters after 31 years," she said with a tired sigh.

"I'm sorry it has been so long," Emerson said. "I can't imagine."

The mermaid nodded silently, staring up through the water toward the star-spangled sky. "I was the first to be sacrificed. My father was an influential merchant who had denied the Shaman a request. Shortly after, the Shaman made an announcement that the Sea had become displeased and required a sacrifice lest it swallow ships and sailors for the next year.

"He explained an elaborate system of selection. His followers hung on his every word and eagerly did his bidding when he announced that I was the Sea's selection." She fell silent, the waves toying with her loose hair. "I was 13."

Emerson's blood heated in anger. "Didn't anyone put up a fuss?"

"Oh, yes, my father did. The followers shut him away until it was over. To save face, the Shaman repeated the selection charade the year after. And every year since…"

"It gives him a sort of power driven by fear," Lilyse added softly, placing a kind arm around Danae's shoulders.

"I wondered why human sacrifice wasn't listed as part of the traditional religion in the *Encyclopedic History of the Cayan Islands*," Emerson muttered through clenched teeth. "He made it all up for control and power."

"So you can see why I'm so interested in bringing him to justice," Danae said. "Is there anything else you need for your plan to work? Anything at all?"

Emerson frowned. "Actually, yes. I have all the supplies and knowledge I need for the invention. But…" he paused. "I haven't yet worked out the problem of needing a boat. One with a net hoist."

The two mermaids exchanged perplexed looks.

"We could steal one from the docks quite easily," Danae said, frowning.

Lilyse looked uncertain. "There must be a better way."

"I have a little money," Emerson said. "I was thinking perhaps someone might rent one to me. I seriously doubt I could hire anyone to help me sail it, though, so I'd need the mermaids' help from below."

Lilyse was shaking her head. "No one will let you take their boat out during the *Hunting Time*, as they call it," she said. "Unless..."

Tugging Danae with her, she turned and zipped away through the water in her unnaturally fast way.

Emerson backed up the shore to see their glows better. They moved away from the island rapidly and then, to his surprise, the glowing became more and more faint.

They're diving down, he realized.

He waited in lonely silence, and a fitful breeze teased his hair.

After a moment, the mermaids' lights reappeared. They parted ways: one headed toward Azul, and another toward him on the coast of Miren.

Lilyse reappeared, swimming smoothly. She smiled at him and opened her hand.

On it lay a heavy golden coin.

INVENTION

The morning air stirred cool and bright around Emerson. He munched a piece of cheese, reminding himself to be careful to chew enough before swallowing. He was having difficulty not just bolting the food.

All the pieces of his grandest invention were laid out before him on the forest floor in tidy rows.

Ready, waiting.

He had spent most of the night mentally assembling the thing over and over. Even in his dreams he had been working on it. Of course, it never worked quite right in his dreams, and he'd woken up more than once feeling anxious.

And a bit stiff from his makeshift bed.

Brushing the feel of the cheese off his fingertips, he got to his feet. Grasping the familiar handle of his hammer, Emerson crouched near the first several pieces of carefully measured wood.

Despite what his dreams had been like, he knew his measurements were perfect and every board would fit exactly as it should. He'd double- and triple-checked.

With satisfying swiftness, the pieces fitted together. The feeling of joy stealing over Emerson as he swung the hammer was only dampened by the circumstances causing the need for this particular invention.

The box began to take shape: about four feet high, three feet wide, and 30 inches deep. It had a solid bottom and no top. Into one of the three-foot sides, he built an opening.

Much to his annoyance, the opening wasn't perfectly square, but that was because neither was the window he'd removed from his workshop wall. The frame was just slightly cock-eyed.

Emerson had made his opening a perfect fit, however. It had to be or the box wouldn't be watertight.

Once the entire box was assembled, he inserted the window. He hoped his mother wouldn't mind that he'd pried it right out of the workshop wall. He had thought to cover the gap with a piece of tar paper to keep out the weather and the ever-curious gulls.

Standing back, Emerson looked over his progress. The box with the window was unlike anything he'd ever seen, and he felt confident something like it had never been invented before.

Just above the window was a round opening. He looked at the pieces still lying on the forest floor. This last step was the most delicate. The success of the whole thing would depend on it.

He sat cross-legged and began the detailed assembly process. It was now far past noon, and he wanted to get this part assembled before it was too dark to see.

This is like a separate invention in and of itself, he thought as he meticulously fitted it together.

Safe and sound at home again
Let the waters roar, Jack
Safe and sound at home again
Let the waters roar, Jack
Long we've tossed on the rolling main
Now we're safe ashore, Jack
Don't forget your old shipmate
Fal dee ral dee ral dee rye eye doe!

Emerson realized he was singing the sea shanty from his dream under his breath. He laid down his tools and stared out toward the water—what he could see through the trees. In the distance, the shape of Azul rose pale grey and rugged from the waves.

Home.

He would be happy to be home when this was all over.

Of course, if my plan doesn't work, I'll probably never be able to go home.

Sobered by the thought and by the sinking sun, Emerson leaned back over the complicated mess of the invention in his lap.

By the time it was dusk, he'd finished assembling the sound device. The concept was similar to the speaking tube. It was simple in design, but complicated to build, especially without the benefit of being in his workshop. In the last of the daylight, he fitted it into the round hole above the box's window and anchored it securely.

His stomach rumbled loudly and he realized he hadn't stopped for a meal since breakfast. Rummaging through his knapsack, he removed the last of his food stores.

Eating silently by the light of the rising crescent moon, Emerson brought out Lilyse's gold coin and gazed at it thoughtfully. It had weighed heavily in his trouser pocket all day, reminding him of what he had to do next.

This part of his plan was incredibly dangerous. His pulse quickened at the thought. The Shaman's men would no doubt still be searching for him. They would know by now they had attacked the wrong lad that night.

He'd have to slip through village unnoticed until he got to the market square. There, the worst he could expect would be jeering and gossip; the Shaman's men wouldn't try and attack him with everyone watching.

Getting away safely afterward would likely be the hardest part... unless Lilyse's gold was enough to secure him the use of a boat. Then, he'd be safe in the company of the boat's owner all the way back to the shore.

Working to convince himself that was the likely outcome and he had nothing to worry about, Emerson licked the last crumbs from his fingers.

His stomach growled again, but there wasn't a scrap of food left. He sighed.

At least I'm going to the market anyway tomorrow.

REQUEST

Emerson patted his pocket for the sixth time. The heavy gold coin was still there. He felt for the ornate knife in his belt. The day he'd picked it up off the ground, he'd only been thinking of keeping it away from the men who'd thrown it at him. Now, he had brought it along as a last defense in case they caught up to him again.

Like a shadow, he slipped through the streets of the village, moving as fast as he dared, constantly checking behind him. He was almost to the market. He crouched in an alleyway and looked over the busy booths.

Toward the east end of the market he spotted a wine-seller. Large kegs with spigots in their ends were stacked behind his booth. Emerson hoped climbing up to the highest one would give him the platform he needed.

His legs felt slightly wobbly as he stood from his crouching position. He took a deep breath and squeezed his eyes shut. This was the last thing he normally wanted to do.

Go to the market.

Make a scene.

Draw attention to himself.

Tell a crazy tale that would have the crowd shaking their heads at best and jeering at worst.

He called up the image of Lilyse floating in the water, semi-transparent and glowing. Her white dress and loose hair rippling in the moving waves. Danae, with her sad eyes and reluctance to even speak after 31 years as a ghost. The hope the 30 mermaids had placed in him.

He tried to swallow the rising feeling of panic, but it barely helped.

I am going to feel it. It's not something I can just wish away.

Emerson opened his eyes. *But I can still do the right thing no matter how it makes me feel.*

He commanded his feet to move.

Purposefully ignoring the people around him, he made it to the wine-seller's booth without even noticing if anyone had looked at him askance. The merchant was busy with a customer, so Emerson didn't even stop to speak to him.

Scaling the wine barrels, he raised himself up to stand on the highest one.

Faces. A sea of them, and several were already looking at him. Little boys pointed, saying indistinct, excited things.

Apparently it's not every day the village lunatic climbs up the wine barrels.

Emerson swallowed hard. He was glad, then, there hadn't been anything for breakfast. More and more faces were turned toward him as people jostled their neighbors and pointed to the strange sight.

Don't start by saying, "Um, hi," he told himself.

"Um, hi." He quavered. *This is already off to a great start.*

He pushed through the quaver until what came out was a shout. "Can I have your attention for just a moment, please? You probably all know there have been some pretty strange rumors going around. I want to explain briefly what's going on, and ask a favor."

The market had gone eerily close to silent. Aside from the murmur of some quieted voices rippling through the crowd, most everyone was listening. The wine merchant was staring up at him in surprise.

Emerson plunged ahead before his knocking knees could get the better of him. "You might know my trade is repairing things, but I also like to try my hand at new inventions."

A man shook his head and muttered something derisive-sounding to his neighbor. Emerson was well aware some in the village thought his inventing was a waste of time. He looked away and continued, trying to keep his voice from wobbling too much.

"I discovered a way to converse with mermaids and invented a tool to help me do so. Since that time, they have told me their story—" a few people laughed

"—They have been trying to ask us for help for years; that's why sailors have always reported their mouths moving as if in speech. You see, they are not mermaids at all, but water-bound ghosts. They will not be able to rest in peace until their killer is brought to justice."

Suddenly, Emerson caught sight of his mother in the crowd. Her face was beaming with pride as she looked at him. Beside her, Cyrus stood grumbling. Idina turned and said something to him, and he quieted.

"Now, you may not believe me, and to be perfectly honest, I wouldn't have believed such a tale either. But then I heard a mermaid speak. I've come up with a way to give others the opportunity to do the same and then decide for themselves. Now, I have something to ask."

The murmuring got a bit louder and was punctuated by occasional laughter as Emerson put his hand into his trouser pocket. He withdrew the heavy coin and held it up high.

"I'm not asking you to help me find justice for the mermaids, and I'm not even asking you to believe me. I'm asking someone to rent me their boat for one day." He flipped the coin, causing it to glint blindingly in the sunlight.

A movement toward the back of the crowd caught his eye and he saw two uncomfortably familiar figures join the others. The Shaman's men had caught wind of what was going on.

I have to make this work.

Otherwise, he would be in even more danger. There was relative silence among the people gathered, but then, like a wave originating at the back of the crowd near the newcomers, negative murmuring swept the market.

People were shaking their heads.

"Daft boy..."

"At hunting time? That's my livelihood..."

"Not for all the gold coins..."

"What, does he take us for fools?"

Emerson involuntarily glanced toward the Shaman's men. They stood silent with their arms folded across their chests. The scar-faced one gave him a taunting nod.

"Well, if you're interested, um—come talk to me," Emerson said over the rising noise in a final effort to make his plea heard.

He quickly got off the barrels before his legs could give out.

DEFENSE

The activity of the market resumed as if nothing had happened. As if the strangest lad in the village hadn't just stood on a stack of wine barrels and asked to rent a boat during the Hunting Time. The only difference now? Nobody was looking at Emerson. Nobody would meet his eyes.

He remained by the wine merchant's booth for a little while, hoping against hope that someone would approach him. Someone who didn't want to volunteer in front of everyone, but would be willing to speak to him about it more privately.

He rubbed his hands together nervously to keep from clenching them.

Just when he was about to turn and leave, someone spoke at his elbow.

"I'm sorry nobody is willing."

He turned to find himself looking down at Saria. She met his eyes sympathetically for a moment before glancing around the crowd. Things were still awkward between them. "It's a hard sell, especially this time of year. But I'm a little surprised nobody is interested in that coin."

Emerson withdrew the coin from his pocket again and gazed at it. "Lilyse found it deep in the sea. She hoped it would convince someone to help me if not for justice, at least for profit."

"What will you do now?" Saria asked after a moment.

Emerson stood up straighter and lifted his chin. "I'll either buy a boat or make one." He looked down at her again and said sadly, "In either case, it will be too late for this year's sacrifice. There will be another 'mermaid' by the time I can put my plan into effect."

Saria lightly touched his hand with her fingertips. He hadn't realized he had begun clenching his fists. Or that they were starting to shake ever so slightly. *Not now...*

"I should go," he said. "Best get to work on that new plan. I'm glad you're feeling better."

Saria nodded, a strange look in her eyes.

Emerson slipped away from the market square. What had Saria's expression meant? He wasn't sure what he'd seen. It was something akin to admiration. He wasn't sure if she'd made up her mind about him yet, but at least they'd spoken—albeit awkwardly.

He paused to catch his breath, panting as he leaned against the back wall of Millie's Pub. It was then he realized he hadn't been running and that he shouldn't be out of breath.

No, no, no, no...

He oozed down the side of the building until he was sitting on the dusty ground. Images he'd pushed away in the moment now flashed into his mind.

Someone jeering.

Someone shaking their head and then whispering.

Cyrus' disapproving face.

Little boys pointing.

And faces—so many faces—all staring at him all at once.

He felt like he couldn't get enough air and his chest ached. He forced his clenched fists open and laid them flat against his drawn-up knees. He breathed in, counting.

One—two—three—four—

He held it and then exhaled as slowly and as measured as he could.

Again.

He untucked his shirt from his trousers and wiped his sweating forehead with the hem.

One—two—three—four—

Again—

But suddenly there was no air to be had. Something had struck his abdomen with nauseating force. Emerson's mouth gaped, searching for breath, and his eyes flew open. He wanted to simultaneously grasp his aching middle and claw at his throat, trying to find air.

He couldn't; his arms were held fast to his sides in a human vise-grip. The darker of the Shaman's men held him fast. The scar-faced man flipped his ornate braids over his shoulder and cocked his head to one side.

"Definitely the right one this time," he said calmly.

"Good," the other man said. "I'm sick of this accursed island. Let's be done with it."

Emerson's breath was returning and he squirmed, kicking and thrashing. He contorted his right arm and after a moment was able to hook it under the edge of his loose shirt.

The scar-faced man looked skyward and shook his head. "One minute you're hiding like a coward and the next you think you're going to somehow wriggle away from two full-grown men? You're a fool, Emerson Kadwell."

Emerson's hand closed over cool metal. Over something the men couldn't see, hidden beneath the shirt he'd untucked just moments before.

The scar-faced man made a move forward. In that moment, with a painful contortion of his wrist, Emerson plunged the ritual knife straight back into flesh. The man behind him howled and loosened his grip.

Everything happened quickly then. Emerson shot forward, blessed air filling his lungs and a heightened survival instinct driving him. The scar-faced man lunged, but missed him by mere inches.

Emerson kicked up dust as he ran faster than he'd ever run before. Twisting to look behind him, he saw the scar-faced man in pursuit while his accomplice doubled over on the ground, clutching a rapidly expanding red stain.

In a wild gamble born of desperation, Emerson twisted and flung the knife at his pursuer. Time seemed to stand still except for the continued pounding of his feet despite the fact he had twisted to look behind him. And the knife: red inlaid handle flipping over reddened metal blade, over and over.

Emerson turned his head forward again and swerved into a street to his left. He didn't see whether, by a great stroke of luck, the knife had found its mark. There was no reason it should—he wasn't skilled with knives in the slightest.

And a part of him hoped it hadn't. The part of him that, despite the danger to himself, never wanted to harm someone ever again. The part that replayed the sickening memory of what he had just been forced to do.

Sometime later he realized he was sitting in his cave, listening to the ebb and flow of the waves. He didn't know how long he had been there, or precisely how he'd arrived. He did know that the sun was sinking, he was utterly exhausted, and that he had failed at procuring a boat.

DAPHNE

Emerson sat on a hard rock at the edge of the woods, staring at his invention. The sun was just cresting the horizon and beginning to filter through the trees, bathing the large wooden box in golden light. He slid another spoonful of cold beans into his mouth.

The beans were all he'd been able to locate in the dark of the cottage the night before. He could tell by feel that he had one of his mother's canning jars, but he had hoped to find it was something more like strawberry preserves.

He shrugged. The meal fit his current mood: not great.

Clink!

Emerson finally broke his reverie and turned to look behind him. For the past several minutes, the strange sound had repeated itself over and over. It had finally become annoying.

"Stupid gull, no doubt," he grunted, standing.

Shuffling down to the sand, he arrived just in time to see a small rock come sailing out of the water and land against a half-submerged boulder.

Clink!

Peering more closely at the bright water, Emerson could just barely discern the mirage-like outline of a mermaid. With as bright as the sunrise was, he couldn't identify which mermaid was throwing things to get his attention.

That was a clever way to do it. The rocks can break through the surface even if she can't!

He put his hand in the water. "One minute!" he said. Then he scrambled back up the beach and to the trees. He grabbed the speaking tube and returned to the water.

"Finally!" Lilyse's voice greeted him, when he'd lowered the device into the water and put it to his ear. "Listen, some of the girls are reporting a boat left the Chadwick docks just before dawn. It's headed this way."

Emerson rubbed the light stubble on his chin in thought. "Could they make out the name?"

I hope the Shaman's men didn't discover I'm staying here on Miren.

"Yes, they said it's called *The Daphne.*"

Emerson felt his mouth drop open. Lilyse laughed at him and he snapped it shut again. "You're sure it's the *Daphne*?"

"Positive. Why? Whose boat is she?"

Emerson was already scrambling up on the boulder, though. Sure enough, there was a fishing boat headed for the coast of Miren.

Something about this didn't make sense. Why was Mr. Beggley sailing to Miren? How did he know where Emerson was? Why hadn't he said something when Emerson had been in town the day before? Emerson frowned. What if it wasn't Mr. Beggley at all? What if someone was coming to take him back to the village— or worse, to the Shaman's men?

Emerson jumped down off the boulder and spoke to Lilyse again. "I don't know what's going on. I'm going to play it safe."

He removed the speaking tube from the water and dashed back into the woods. From cover, he watched as the boat loomed larger. The deck seemed deserted, but for one figure at the helm. He couldn't quite make out who it was, but it almost looked like Ned—the man who'd worked with him on the fence.

The boat came in as close as it could and dropped its anchor. The figure at the helm turned and spoke to someone Emerson couldn't see from where he stood.

A moment later, a feminine figure left the boat and splashed through the shallows.

Saria?!

Emerson left his hiding place in the woods. Saria caught sight of him and waved. She trudged up the sand, her russet-red skirts made dark and heavy by the sea water.

Emerson jogged forward to reach her. "What are you doing here?" he asked. "What's going on? How did you find me?"

Saria laughed breathlessly and pushed stray hair from her face. "So many questions! What am I doing here? I've brought you a boat! What's going on? Again—I've brought you a boat. Use it! How did I find you? I had a lovely chat with your mother. Mr. Hammer seemed to think I was a spy or something, but you know how he can be..."

She smiled broadly at his surprise.

He stared at her for a moment before what she'd done fully registered. He ran his fingers through his hair nervously. "Wow. Saria, I don't know what to say..."

"Thank you?" she asked, pretty pink spots blossoming in her cheeks.

"Yes, of course that. And thank you for believing me and—and trusting me to not slap away your friendship," he said. Emerson was suddenly acutely aware of her height—or lack thereof, the way her hair smelled like vanilla, the light freckles on the bridge of her nose. He'd never noticed them.

Her eyes were green. Or blue. Maybe grey?

"What now?" she asked.

"Does your father—?"

"No, he doesn't know anything about this. I bribed Ned into helping me. Promised him a pie."

So that is *Ned.*

He shook his head. "You're something else, Saria."

"Why, thank you," she said pertly.

"Get Ned to come ashore, and I'll explain my plan," he said.

BOX

Emerson led Saria and Ned into the woods. They silently took in his rustic campsite, the tools and scraps scattered about, and the strange wooden box covered in pitch with a window and round communication device in the side.

Ned walked all the way around the box, silently observing. Saria asked, "What is it, Emerson?"

"I'm going to show the villagers a mermaid. Let them hear her story for themselves. It's the only thing that will convince them."

Saria's eyes widened. Ned had stopped to listen, cupping his good ear to make out what Emerson was saying.

"So you want to use the net hoist?" he asked loudly.

"You've got the right idea," Emerson said, delighted the man had already caught on.

Saria looked a little puzzled, and she asked, "You're going to lower that into the sea with the net hoist?"

"Yes, and then Lilyse can get inside. When we hoist it back up, she will still be in sea water, technically, but everyone will be able to see and hear her."

"That's brilliant, Emerson!" Saria said. Then she frowned. "We have to wait until it's dark, though, don't we?"

"Or nearly dark, yes. They're almost impossible to see in the daylight."

"You say, *almost*..." Saria said.

Emerson grinned. "Come on, I'll see if she's still in the shallows."

Saria beckoned to Ned. "Could you bring the picnic basket from the boat, please?" she asked loudly for his benefit.

"Of course!" he said. "I'll be back in a jiffy."

Emerson groaned. "You have food?"

Saria gave him a strange look. "Yes...? Have you not eaten?"

"Not unless a few spoonfuls of cold beans count."

She looked at him sympathetically. "I'll get you all taken care of."

Emerson retrieved his speaking tube and showed Saria how it worked. He waded into the waves and searched for a glimpse of Lilyse or one of the other mermaids. "Lilyse, are you still around?" he asked.

In response, something grabbed his ankle. He jerked back and shouted, nearly toppling into the water.

Saria yelped in surprise.

"Knock it off, Lilyse," he said. "You want her to be afraid of you?"

He put the speaking tube to his ear so he could hear her reply. "No, not really," she said contritely. "You two are adorable, by the way."

"Stop it," he growled. "Mind your manners and say hello."

He handed the speaking tube to Saria. She listened intently for a moment, her eyes growing wider and wider.

"Why, hello! I—I can't see where you are, but I can hear you!" she spoke excitedly into the tube. After another moment of listening, she said to Emerson. "She says if you stand just there, you will cast a shadow in the water right in front of me. Maybe then I'll be able to see her a little."

Emerson moved through the shallow water to stand where she'd indicated. Sure enough, in the shadow he cast, they could just make out Lilyse. She waved, giving Saria a little smile.

"There you are!" Saria gasped. "It's so nice to see you!" She sobered. "I'm terribly sorry for everything you've been through. I hope that with my father's boat, Emerson can make everything right."

The mermaid spoke to Saria for a moment. Emerson couldn't hear what she said, but he had a feeling, from the way Saria glanced up and smiled at him, his name had been mentioned. He felt his face grow warm and he looked away.

Ned was just setting the picnic basket on the sand, far out of the reach of the waves. Emerson pointed this out to Saria.

Half an hour later, Emerson was feeling better than he had in a while, as he realized. "It's been a long time since I've had a meal this good," he groaned.

Saria looked pleased.

Are her cheeks always that pink or...?

He shook himself. "There's work to be done."

While Saria packed up the dinner things, he showed Ned that he'd attached runners to the underside of the box. "We can push it down to the water. It will be slow going at first, but once we get to hard-packed sand, it should move pretty smoothly."

He waved Saria over. "Ready to help us push this thing?" he asked.

She nodded determinedly.

They arranged themselves at the back of the box and began walking it forward. As Emerson had predicted, it moved sluggishly at first.

Emerson suddenly became aware that the back of Saria's head was just in front and to the left of him. Her brown curls were braided into a coil at the base of her neck. Shiny, soft tendrils escaped here and there, waving gently in the sea breeze.

Focus, Emerson.

He frowned and pushed harder on the box. They were almost to the hard-packed sand. In another moment they reached it, and the box slid with much greater speed and ease.

They pushed it right into the lapping waves.

"I'll get the hoist," Saria said, plunging forward. Emerson and Ned waited by the box. Atop the boat, Saria turned a large crank, causing a hook and cable to lower down the side of the boat. Emerson ran forward and attached it securely to a network of strong ropes he had added to the box's design.

Emerson felt a profound sense of gratitude that this moment was happening.

Ned joined Saria, and together they turned the crank the other way, slowly pulling the box toward the boat. Emerson went with it, guiding it. He stopped when it had reached the side of the boat. Letting the floating box tip to the side, he allowed it to fill with water. It sank slowly.

"Lilyse," he called into his speaking tube, "come have a look."

The water next to him rippled and shifted. She was there.

"It's incredible, Emerson," her voice said, coming quietly through the speaking tube. "And it's a great fit."

He squinted, trying to see her. She was just barely visible in the slightly darkened interior of the box. "I'm glad," he said. "We will leave just before sundown."

Emerson scrambled onto the fishing boat. Now the waiting began.

MOB

The air had quickly turned cool as the sun dipped below the shining water and turned the sky a fiery orange. The sea breeze rippled through Emerson's shirt and chilled him. Beside him, Saria shivered.

"Cold?" he asked.

"No," she answered, not turning her face from the approaching shore of Azul. "Nervous, I think." After a moment, she glanced up at him, searching his face.

"I think I am, too," he told her, removing his hands from his pockets and looking at them.

Saria turned her attention toward his hands as well. He tried to hold them still, especially under her gaze, but they still shook just slightly. He pocketed them again, ashamed she'd seen, and looked toward the island.

After a moment, Saria laid a hand on his arm, and he felt himself relax inside just a little.

These feelings of panic were something he'd never had control over, but this remarkable girl had helped just by reminding him she was there. He looked down at her, standing by his side, and prayed his plan would succeed.

Ned expertly piloted the boat to within a few yards of the nearest dock and then dropped the anchor.

"Oh, my," Saria said quietly, leaving Emerson's side and going forward.

A crowd of villagers was gathered along the fence. The more daring men had crossed the fence and were on the docks. The sunset illuminated a sea of tense faces.

"Ho there!" someone called.

"Papa?" Saria answered. "I'm here! I'm all right!" She waved.

Mr. Beggley pushed through the crowd and came to the nearest dock. "What is the meaning of this?" he demanded. "I've been worried out of my mind. My daughter and my fishing boat missing since early this morning!" He rubbed his forehead.

"Hey, that's Emerson Kadwell!" someone from the crowd shouted.

Emerson winced but forced himself to stand tall.

Mr. Beggley's head snapped up. "What is this? Did you take my boat and my daughter?" His face creased with fury.

"No, sir—" Emerson began.

"Papa, I took the boat out to Emerson. It was entirely my doing."

"Rubbish!" Mr. Beggley boomed. "You know nothing about sailing!"

"You'd be surprised!" Saria fired back. "But, yes, I got someone to help me."

"Well, young lady, tell whoever is helping you to bring my hanged boat up to this dock immediately!"

Saria whispered to Emerson, "He must have been sick with worry. Papa is never this cross." She turned and shook her head at Ned.

"I'm sorry, Papa," she said more loudly. "I can't do that. Emerson has something important to discuss with everyone, and until he's had the opportunity, we will stand off from the docks."

She looked up at Emerson encouragingly. He took a deep breath.

"You might have heard what I said in the market yesterday," he said, hoping his voice carried over the creaking of the anchored boats and the rushing waves. "I told you I would have found the mermaids' story hard to believe if I hadn't heard it straight from them. Today, I intend to give you the same opportunity."

Voices rose up from the crowd, answering indistinctly. Fear and anger rolled off them in waves.

"You're a fool, Emerson Kadwell!" someone shouted above the murmuring.

"Has he gone from pestering our governor to kidnapping?"

"He would have us all go swimming with the mermaids!"

The next voice to call out seemed slightly familiar to Emerson. "He needs to be stopped!"

In the failing light, he couldn't see who had spoken, but something in his gut told him it was the scar-faced man. The crowd didn't seem to care who had suggested this or what their motives might be, for they took up the suggestion immediately.

Someone was handing out torches, and the faces illuminated by their flickering lights were drawn in fear and distrust.

"Someone get a hook!"

"We'll pull that boat right in!"

"Saria, please!" a woman's voice called. The crowd quieted just slightly and then gasped in horror as a woman climbed awkwardly over the fence and came shakily down the wooden dock. "Saria, it's me, Madge. Please just bring the boat in and come home. I'm not sure what Emerson needs, but I'm sure your father can help him if only you'll come home and talk to him about it."

Mr. Beggley hurried to meet their housekeeper. "Go back to the fence, Madge. It's not at all safe out here."

"But, sir, they're going to drag your boat in and I'm afraid of what—"

The rest of their words were drowned out by the loud voices of the crowd as several men jumped the fence. They carried a grappling hook and a long coil of rope.

The noise level surged, and Emerson's stomach clenched as he realized the crowd had just turned into a mob.

CHAOS

The men with the grappling hook came to the very end of the dock, much to the fright of the other villagers. "Do you want me to try to move the boat out of reach?" Ned asked Emerson, as quietly as the half-deaf man was able.

Before Emerson could reply, the dock shuddered violently, sending the men sprawling into one another and scrambling to keep from falling into the water.

The water. Where everyone had forgotten to look.

Half a dozen faint mermaid glows were clustered around the support posts of the dock they had just rammed. Emerson looked behind them. Sure enough, mermaids were streaming into the Chadwick harbor, their glowing becoming ever more visible in the dim light remaining after the sunset.

The villagers were speaking amongst themselves in panic-stricken voices, and the men with the grappling hook had backed up toward the beach. They conferred quietly about what to do. Mr. Beggley hurried Madge off the dock and back to the far side of the fence.

Someone in the crowd hurled a curse and the villagers began raising their voices once more. The men on the dock crept forward.

"I need you to trust me for a moment," Emerson called out. "There's no risk. I only want to let you see and hear the truth about the mermaids."

"You've had enough chances! We've allowed more than enough of this!" someone shouted. Several other voices agreed.

"So you're that afraid of the truth?" Emerson asked. He knew he was provoking them, but at the moment he didn't particularly care.

"We're only afraid of losing our livelihood because of you!"

The man holding the grappling hook threw it. It caught on the edge of the *The Daphne* with a dull thud. Before the men could take up the slack in the rope, the mermaids surrounding the dock rammed the support posts again, causing it to shudder once more.

At the same time, the other fishing boats in the harbor began bucking and thrashing, knocking together with dull thuds. The crowd grew instantly quiet, frozen in shock. Then, fearful murmuring ran throughout the assembly.

"It's the mermaids!" a woman shrieked.

Emerson could see clearly now that it was almost completely dark: mermaids had swarmed around the boats and were rocking and shoving them. He had a hunch they were buying him time. And possibly giving him a bargaining tool.

"I will ask the mermaids why they're attacking your boats," he said loudly. "Do not attempt to pull us in."

A collective gasp ran through the people gathered beyond the fence.

Emerson bent over the edge of the boat, lowered the speaking tube into the water, and asked quietly, "Lilyse, what are the mermaids doing?" He put it to his ear and listened. After a moment, he stood up.

"She says they want you to listen to what I have to say. Unless everyone clears off the dock and lets me explain with no further trouble, the mermaids say they will wreck every boat docked here. Those are their requirements."

The men on the dock moved back slowly, their faces wearing heavy scowls. The crowd muttered angrily. The boats immediately stilled and the mermaids backed off a few feet.

"I know it's unpleasant to have your ships held hostage, but think about how desperate they must be to do something like this. You will understand once you know their story." He couldn't tell if his words had much of an effect on the crowd, but they had settled down some—if only to save their livelihood.

He signaled to Ned and Saria. They went to the crank that operated the net hoist. "There have been men looking for me ever since I spoke to the governor. I believe they're standing among you tonight, even. Because of this, I left the island on a homemade raft. I brought supplies and tools with me to the island of Miren. For several days now, I have been secretly

191

working on an invention that will allow you all to hear the mermaids' story."

He joined Ned and Saria at the net hoist. Together, they turned the crank until the box rose out of the water.

"This is my invention," Emerson called to the crowd. "It is a water-tight box that holds sea water. I've fitted it with a window so you can see the mermaid and a sound device that will allow you to hear her."

"What mermaid?" someone called rudely, tauntingly.

"So you *are* ready for the truth, then?" Emerson fired back.

For once, the crowd was silent. Nobody answered. Together, the three on the boat lowered the box into the waves once more.

Just below, in the dark water, Lilyse smiled up at them. She was ready to tell her story.

MADGE

The hoist groaned as they lowered the box back into the water. As soon as it was well beneath the surface, Lilyse swam up to the top of the box and then down into the water inside. She looked up and gave them a wave.

Reversing the direction of the crank, Emerson, Ned, and Saria hauled the box up the side of the ship. Emerson watched anxiously as the top of the box broke the surface of the water. Lilyse, still safely ensconced in the sea water the box held smiled up at him reassuringly.

When the ropes at the top of the box were within reach, Emerson tugged on them to make the whole thing turn. He needed the window and sound device to face the crowd of villagers on the shore.

With the darkness that had settled over the gathering since the sun went down, Lilyse's glow shone brightly, and she was distinctly visible through the box's window.

The crowd gasped.

Anyone who was standing outside the fence scrambled back over.

Emerson gave Lilyse a nod. It was her turn to speak.

I do hope the sound device works correctly. It does in theory, but... everything hinges on this.

Nobody but he and Saria had ever heard a mermaid speak. This was going to astonish everyone.

If it worked.

The crowd waited in tense silence.

"Hello," Lilyse said, her voice coming through loudly enough, but with a slightly muffled quality. Emerson sagged with relief. He heard Saria let out a pent-up breath behind him. A murmur ran through the crowd. They quickly fell silent, however, waiting for her to say more.

"I once lived on the island of Stron Cay in a small village. On Stron Cay, Shaman Orith has a tradition of making a yearly sacrifice to the sea. He calls it the Sea Appeasement. He tells his followers that, without it, there will be more drownings, more ships lost, fewer catches.

"I was selected as the sacrifice the year I turned 15. The Shaman's men took me from my mother and back to his village. There, the Shaman brought me out in his ritual boat where they drowned me as the sacrifice." Lilyse spoke plainly and bluntly.

Emerson heard several women gasp. For the most part, it seemed many in the crowd were either still too dumbfounded or were withholding judgement to have much of a reaction.

"This all happened 20 years ago," Lilyse said. "The practice started 10 years before that with a young girl named Danae. She was the daughter of a merchant with whom Shaman Orith had a quarrel. In retaliation, the Shaman concocted this story about the sea needing an appeasement sacrifice. To save face and to keep the power it gives him over his followers, he has continued the practice these last 30 years. That's why there are 30 mermaids."

Lilyse glanced over at Emerson. He stepped to the bow of the boat and said, "The truth about the mermaids is that they're the ghosts of girls unjustly killed by Shaman Orith to maintain his power and influence. They will only find rest when he is brought to justice. Until then, they're bound to the water in which they died."

"This is what we've been trying to explain to you these many years," Lilyse added. "We were asking for help, but no one could hear us. We are truly sorry for frightening you."

The crowd shuffled uncertainly and in that moment, a voice called out. "This is some kind of trick. The Shaman is a highly respected man. Come now, Emerson: how did you do it? What's the real secret of your invention?"

Emerson squinted toward the torchlit crowd, trying to single out the speaker. He had a feeling he knew who it was. He had just made out the head and shoulders of the scar-faced man standing at the back of the crowd, his Cayan partner hunched over a bandaged stomach—when someone shrieked and a commotion broke out.

"What happened?" Saria asked, coming to his side.

Emerson shook his head uncertainly. "I'm not sure. I was looking at something else."

The villagers all faced toward something going on in the center of the crowd. It appeared a woman had fainted. Several people knelt around her. From the boat, Emerson and Saria couldn't make out who it was. The fence and the crowd blocked most of their view of whoever was on the ground.

After a moment, the woman seemed to come to, because the crowd relaxed and backed off a little. Mr. Beggley helped her up and Emerson and Saria gasped together, "Madge?"

Lilyse knocked on the wooden box and Emerson went to speak to her.

"What happened?" she asked.

Emerson touched the top of the water in the box and said, "A woman fainted, although I'm not exactly sure why. She's the Beggleys' housekeeper, Madge."

Lilyse started, and she stared up at Emerson with enormous eyes. "What did you say?" she whispered.

BELIEF

"Madge fainted," Emerson repeated, confused by Lilyse's sudden intensity. He looked up as raised voices reached his ears.

The housekeeper seemed to have recovered quickly. She climbed awkwardly over the fence despite Mr. Beggley's pleading objections. He followed her as she hurried down the beach and toward the dock.

"What do you mean? How is that possible?" he asked. "You really should sit down, Madge."

"No," she said loudly, her voice thick with emotion. "I'm telling you, that's my daughter—just how she looked 20 years ago when the Shaman's men took her from me back on Stron Cay—and I *am* going to speak with her."

Behind her, the villagers gasped and murmured to each other. Emerson could see looks of horror dawning over many faces as they realized what Madge's statement entailed. His and Lilyse's story had just been validated to them all by a well-loved and respected member of the community. Emerson felt his heart swell with hope even as it broke for the Beggleys' housekeeper.

Saria was frozen, staring at him in open-mouthed surprise. He went to her quickly.

"She never said much about her life before coming to Azul. I always knew she'd lost her family somehow, but—" Saria looked ready to cry for the woman who had, in many ways, been a mother to her in the years since her own mother's death.

Together they looked down toward the box, anchored to the side of the ship. Lilyse's hand covered her mouth in shock as she watched her mother come down the dock.

Madge and Mr. Beggley conversed quietly for a moment. "Will you bring the boat in now?" he called. He swept his hand toward the crowd, huddled together in shock, still trying to process the unthinkable tale they now knew to be true. "I don't think anyone—least of all me—is interested in causing you any trouble."

Emerson looked at Saria, and she nodded. She knew her father was sincere. In this moment, everyone wanted one thing: to reunite mother and daughter.

They weighed the anchor, and Ned guided the boat the last several yards, bringing the mermaid's box to eye-level with the two standing on the dock.

Madge and Lilyse stared at each other through the window for several moments. Finally, Lilyse said, "Hello, mother."

Madge began crying softly.

Emerson turned away. "You should go explain to Madge how to reply," he said, handing Saria the speaking tube.

"So, it's true?" called a voice from the crowd.

"Every word of it," Emerson replied, leaving the boat for the dock. He walked slowly toward the end of the dock and the crowd of villagers clustered on the other side of the fence.

"And we don't actually need to fear the mermaids? They don't drag sailors under and drown them?" a woman asked, her voice still tinged with fear.

"No," Emerson said, almost laughing. "They don't. It's quite the opposite in my experience. I think you're all aware that I nearly drowned when I was a small child. Were there rumors it was a mermaid?"

The crowd shifted uneasily and nobody replied. Emerson took that as confirmation.

"Well, it *was* a mermaid—who saved my life that day. Lilyse calmed me with a song and carried me back to the safety of the shore, pushing me up out of the waves."

"They need justice, there's no doubt about that!" a young man said hotly.

The crowd agreed loudly.

Groups of people can be so fickle! One minute, they're a mob after me for being a trouble-maker and then next minute— oh, no!

"Look around you," Emerson said, suddenly in a hurry. "Do you see two men: a Cayan wearing a bandage, and a red-haired man with a large scar? They're both wearing the braids of the Shaman's followers. They need to be found before they alert the Shaman to what's going on!"

Angry-sounding voices swept the crowd.

"I remember seeing those two in the market!"

"That sounds like the men who beat my nephew!"

"Where are they now?"

"No ambassadors of the Shaman should be allowed here anymore!"

"Maybe the Shaman and his men should be killed—his crimes certainly deserve it!"

Emerson shouted above the noise. "No! You can't just go over and execute him! Would that be justice?" The crowd fell into a sullen silence.

"A lynching isn't justice. And I'm afraid because of that, you'd just doom the mermaids to being ghosts forever. The Shaman *and* his men need to be properly tried and sentenced by the courts on Stron Cay."

Several sailors were nodding in begrudging agreement.

Villagers are listening to me. Taking me seriously. Agreeing.

Emerson's head spun with the sudden changes. But it wasn't just because of the changes. He suddenly felt overwhelmingly exhausted. He rubbed his face and leaned against a large post at the beginning of the dock.

In an instant, his mother was at his side, having crossed the fence despite Cyrus' protestations. "You've done well, Emerson. Come home and rest."

"No, Mum." He shook his head and pushed away from the post determinedly. "I'm not finished. I have to see this through. I have to go to Stron Cay."

Mr. Beggley had approached just then, leaving Madge's side for the first time since she'd seen her daughter. "I agree something must be done. I am prepared to take you, Madge, and Lilyse across to Stron Cay in the morning."

Emerson sighed in relief. "Thank you, Mr. Beggley. You have no idea how much I appreciate it. Unfortunately, I don't know that we can afford to wait until the morning. The Shaman could take out his ritual boat anytime now."

Mr. Beggley scowled. "Of course! Hang it all, we do need to hurry. I assume we can take the contraption with Lilyse in it?"

Emerson nodded.

"Good, let me gather a couple of the sailors I typically hire. We will go as fast as the winds will take us."

Emerson tried to hide a smile. "Actually," he said, "I think we can go even faster than that."

Mr. Beggley raised an eyebrow. "Don't tell me you've made some kind of modification to my boat...?"

"Oh, no!" Emerson said hastily. "The mermaids... they don't quite interact with the water normally, and because of that, they're able to move through it unnaturally fast. They've pushed my homemade raft between here and Miren at least a dozen times."

Mr. Beggley nodded. "It's certainly a strange way of gaining speed, but if they're willing and it won't harm *The Daphne...*"

"Promise me you'll try to sleep on the way over, Emrie?" his mother said. He nodded.

"And eat something more," Saria added, patting his arm. "It's been a while since we ate what I brought over."

"Aren't you coming?" Emerson asked. He felt his face flush in the darkness.

Well, that sounded needy.

She shook her head a bit dolefully. Emerson was surprised by how disappointed he felt.

STRON CAY

Emerson woke. For a moment, he wondered where he was and why it smelled so much like fish and wood and pitch. Then he remembered everything: the overnight crossing from Azul to Stron Cay. By the time everything was ready, it was quite late, and he'd fallen asleep the minute he'd stretched out on a rough, folded blanket.

The mermaids had born them across the waves faster than any of the sailors had ever experienced. Now the darkness was just turning to the pale grey before dawn. The boat was rocking gently rather than speeding through the dark water.

Emerson sat up. Pinpricks of light illuminated a large dark mass before them.

We're here. We're actually anchored in Stron Harbor.

He strained to see through the darkness, trying to make out more details of the city. He had never been to Stron Cay.

His stomach rumbled, and he reached for the apple someone had handed him the night before. He had eaten a little before falling asleep, but had tucked the apple into his coat pocket for later. It was all such a sleepy blur.

Mr. Beggley approached. "I see you're awake. Good. What do we need to do to get the contraption ready for transport?"

Emerson blinked slowly. He hadn't thought of them trying to transport Lilyse in the box over land. So far, he had only used it where it could be raised and lowered into the water.

"I will need to double-check its water-tightness. And I'd better rig up a cover for the window unless you want all of Stron getting wind of who we've brought. Otherwise, we will need to hire a team of oxen."

"Madge and I will take care of securing that and an audience with the governor while you work on the box," Mr. Beggley said. Madge nodded tensely.

"I'll hurry. We don't have any time to lose since we don't know when Shaman Orith plans to make this year's sacrifice."

Mr. Beggley agreed. He instructed two of his sailors to hoist the box out of the water at Emerson's direction.

Emerson looked over the side of the boat. Lilyse floated calmly alongside. The others would be waiting a little further out to sea as had been arranged. They hadn't wanted to panic the inhabitants of Stron before Emerson could explain everything to the governor.

When Lilyse saw him, she swam closer to the surface. He leaned down, lowering the speaking tube into the water. "It's almost time," he told her. "I'm going to make a quick modification to the box. When we lower it again, you can get inside."

She nodded. "Thank you for what you're doing, Emerson. Know that Governor Milus has a reputation for being a fair man. He will likely be easier to talk to than Governor Aldan was."

Emerson gave her a wan smile. "I certainly hope so." His stomach clenched just at the thought. He looked over to the sailors who had joined him in looking down into the water. Lilyse gave them a wave and they jumped.

Still getting used to the idea of friendly mermaids, apparently, Emerson thought. He carefully controlled his face so his amusement wouldn't show.

"Let's bring that box up," he said, jerking his head toward the net hoist.

"We've got it, lad," they said. Emerson stepped back and watched with a little envy as they operated the hoist, quickly hauling the heavy box from the water. Their biceps bulged and they hardly seemed to be working at turning the crank.

But as his box became visible in the grey morning light, his heart swelled with pride. Not everyone had the physical strength the sailors had. But then, not everyone had the skill to invent something that had helped change an entire village's mind.

He smiled quietly to himself as the box stopped within arm's reach. He nodded to the sailors and they secured the hoist. Standing back, they watched as he inspected what he could from the deck.

Emerson looked around and located a simple rope ladder. Tossing it over the side, he climbed down carefully, acutely aware of the water below him. Hanging on with one hand, he reached down and made contact with the moving waves so Lilyse could hear him.

"You'll catch me if I fall in, right?" He grinned.

She just rolled her eyes and smiled.

Clinging to the rope ladder, he finished inspecting the rest of the box. Everything seemed to be holding up well. Satisfied, he climbed back up the ladder.

"Do you have any extra sailcloth?" he asked the sailors. "Just a small bit would do: maybe 2 feet square? I need to make a cover for the box's window."

"Sure," one of them said. "I'll be back."

He disappeared down a hatch. The other said, "You really think Governor Milus will be able to stop Shaman Orith?"

"I certainly hope so," Emerson said, pushing back the weariness that threatened to seep through his bones. "Otherwise, all this..."

The sailor nodded soberly. "Well, for what it's worth I have a lot of respect for the lengths you've gone to."

Emerson suddenly didn't know what to say. Something seemed to glow deep inside him. Just then, the other man returned with the sailcloth he'd requested. So, instead of having to use words, Emerson just gave a grateful nod in acknowledgement.

Acceptance.

Respect.

These things were new coming from anyone other than his mother. And—now that he understood her, Saria.

As he went back down the ladder and tacked the cloth across the box's window, his mind wandered. To the village girl who had always been there, on the fringes of his life where he had kept her. He wondered what would have been different if he'd embraced friendship with her all this time.

From the way the last several days had gone and the taste of it he'd had—it would have been a pretty nice thing to have in his life.

He couldn't wait to get home...

"Emerson!" Mr. Beggley's voice sliced through his thoughts. He startled and dropped the hammer he'd been using. It punctured the water with a *plop*.

Quick as a flash, Lilyse retrieved it and held it up to him, a knowing smirk on her face.

Blazes, I'd better not be blushing...

"Yes, Mr. Beggley?" he said, quickly scaling the ladder and hoisting himself back into the boat.

"I've found us an oxcart and team to rent, but... Governor Milus' secretary won't give us an audience today."

Emerson stared at him silently for a moment, his blood hammering in his ears.

What are we going to do now?

TESTIMONY

No audience with Governor Milus. The governor of Stron Cay was bound to be a much busier man than Governor Aldan of Azul. That meant there could be a delay of days, maybe.

Too long. We can't afford to wait.

Something in Emerson's gut told him the time of sacrifice was going to be soon. And the way Madge's face had crumpled at the news bolstered his determination. There had to be some way to force the governor's secretary to fit them into his schedule.

The sunrise was nearly upon them, and in the pale light, he could see a man with a team of oxen waiting on the other side of Stron's fence. A small crowd had gathered as well, shocked to see a new ship in their port.

Nobody travelled the sea this time of year.

Peering over the edge of the boat, Emerson realized it was still just dark enough to see Lilyse clearly glowing in the water.

"I have an idea!" he said to Mr. Beggley. The older man looked surprised but waited in silence.

"Lilyse!" Emerson said hurriedly through the speaking tube. "Bring them all into the harbor. Every last one! Hurry!"

"Everyone but Danae and one other—they're keeping an eye on the Shaman's docks." Lilyse said, and then sped away through the water.

Emerson gripped the side of the boat, leaning forward and looking out toward the sea. It was a race, now, against the rising sun.

But the mermaids could move through the water faster than anything he had ever seen. In a moment, their glows appeared—28 of them. They swarmed around the boat, lighting up the harbor.

The small crowd of people on the other side of the fence gasped and several ran toward the city, screaming unintelligible words.

Emerson grinned at the others.

The governor won't be able to help but hear we've arrived.

Sure enough, a short time later, a messenger pushed his way to the front of the crowd and called across the fence. "Who are you and what are you here for?"

"Theus Beggley and company, and we need to speak with Governor Milus about an urgent matter," Mr. Beggley answered.

"I'm authorized to grant you audience immediately," the messenger said.

The sailors lowered the box into the water at a signal from Emerson. The first ray of sun stabbed across the water, lighting it a blinding gold. Emerson could barely see Lilyse as she slipped into the submerged box. They hoisted the box once more and moved the boat alongside one of the docks.

Emerson watched as Mr. Beggley disembarked and convinced the oxcart owner—through the persuasion of some gold coins—that it was safe to bring his team past the fence.

Gripping his speaking tube and pulling his cap down over his wild hair, Emerson watched as they carefully lowered the box onto the cart. The oxen shifted impatiently.

He felt the same. *Can't we just get to the governor's office? I'm ready for this part to be over.*

A knot was tightening in his stomach. At least he'd only eaten an apple so far today.

Governor Milus was probably a very good poker player, Emerson had decided. All throughout his account and Madge's testimony, the lean, grey-haired man had leaned forward, interestedly taking in their words but betraying nothing of his own thoughts.

Emerson tried desperately to read the governor. Whether he was about to get laughed out of this office as well.

The man leaned back in his regal chair. He looked over to the secretary standing in the wings. "Why did you deny these people audience?" he asked quietly.

The man blinked rapidly. "Well, sir, I didn't know the nature of the issue. The man who inquired didn't explain all this."

"Good on him," the governor said, grimly. "This is a matter that should be kept quiet for the time being. Not told to just anybody."

Emerson's heart dropped.

No.

Governor Milus got stiffly to his feet. "The Shaman is popular with many on this island, and there would be no short supply of people to assist him in hiding from the law should word of these accusations be spread."

Emerson's head spun. *He believes us, then?*

"Word has it you've brought some kind of large, mysterious box on an oxcart. If it contains what I think it does, I'd like to see it immediately."

Emerson swallowed and licked his lips. "We will need to show you in a place that is semi-dark. May we pull into your stables?"

"Of course," the governor said, giving him a serious nod.

They left the governor's office as a group and walked to the nearby stables. The oxcart followed with the box which the sailors had been watching over.

Once inside the dim stable, they asked the oxcart owner and stablehands to leave and closed the double doors. Prying up the nails holding the sailcloth in place, Emerson pulled away the cover from the window.

Everyone looked to the governor in silence. He didn't appear startled, but instead stared levelly at Lilyse, glowing in the water held in Emerson's box. She returned his gaze with a gentle smile and hopeful eyes.

"Hello, Your Excellency," she said, her voice coming through the sound device above the window.

The governor jumped ever so slightly, but his face remained unperturbed.

I really do feel sorry for his fellow poker players.

"Thank you for listening to my friends. Will you help us?" she asked, placing a palm against the inside of the window.

Emerson could feel the pride and sadness rolling off Madge as she watched her daughter. Everyone waited in hopeful, tense silence for the governor's reply.

"Yes," he finally said. "I am hereby launching an official investigation into the Shaman's activities and as many of his followers as were directly involved in the alleged crime."

He turned to Emerson and extended his hand. "Good work, young man."

The proper response lodged somewhere in Emerson's throat, but the keen governor seemed to understand. He gave him an approving smile before turning to shake hands with Mr. Beggley and Madge.

With a thud, one of the stablehands burst through the closed doors of the stable. "Sir! I'm sorry sir, but—there's word that mermaids are attacking all the boats in the harbor! WHAT ON EARTH IS—!" Mr. Beggley's sailors caught the distraught young man as his knees buckled at the sight of Lilyse in the box.

"What is going on?" Governor Milus demanded.

Emerson's stomach roiled. "Something really bad if the mermaids are shaking the boats to get our attention." He had a feeling he knew what it was.

NEWS

"Something's happening down at the harbor," Emerson told Lilyse through the speaking tube. To the others gathered in the stable, he said, "I have to go see what's happened. Follow behind with Lilyse on the oxcart." He hurried out the double doors and yelled over his shoulder, "Don't forget to cover the window again!"

His feet beating a rhythm into the cobblestone streets of Stron, he made his way quickly toward the shore.

No, no, no, no!

They were already too late. He could feel it.

The Shaman must be making his move... and we've only just gotten the governor's word. There's no way his deputies will get there in time.

His heart squeezed in anguish. It was important to him to help the ghosts of previous years finally find justice and rest, but even moreso he had hoped to save the life of whichever girl was to be the Shaman's latest victim.

He ground his teeth and sped faster through the streets.

A fearful crowd had gathered along Stron's fence, but he pushed his way past and went through the opening that had been made to allow the oxcart passage earlier.

Sure enough, every boat in the harbor was rattling and knocking about, just as they had in the Chadwick harbor back home. It was the only way the mermaids could get the attention of those on shore.

Dashing into the waves lapping on the beach—much to the shock of the crowd—Emerson searched the bright water for any signs of a mermaid nearby. The minute he entered the water, the boats stilled.

A murmur of fearful surprise rose up behind him.

There. He spotted the transparent ripple that must be one of the mermaids. Plunging his speaking tube into the water, he asked what was going on.

"Emerson Kadwell? This is Susette." He couldn't be sure, but he thought the mirage under the water waved a greeting. "Danae sent me. The Shaman's men returned a short time ago from the island of Azul. They must have brought a sacrifice with them, for they are now preparing to launch his ritual boat!"

Emerson's heart froze and then restarted with a slow, agonizing pounding.

"How long ago was this?" Emerson asked.

"It took me just a quarter of an hour to come 'round the island," the mermaid's voice replied. "Is the governor sending deputies?"

"Yes," Emerson replied. "He's decided to open an investigation, but there's no way they will be able to make it in time to save the sacrifice."

He bit his lip and stared across the open water. He was going to have to do something himself. The rest of his party wouldn't even make it to the shore soon, since they had the oxcart and box to worry about.

Can I really stop the Shaman all by myself? He clenched his fists. *But if I don't, some innocent girl will die. All I can do is try.*

Thinking fast, he said, "Susette! Gather all the mermaids. I'm going to need you all to take me there as fast as you can." He looked around. "There!" Planting the speaking tube in the sand for his friends to use when they arrived, he raced through the waves and launched himself into a small rowboat.

He fumbled with the rope, his hands clumsy from being in such a hurry. *Hang it all!*

He finally got it untied. Somebody from the crowd by the fence yelled at him, but he ignored them. Emerson grasped the oars, giving one strong pull.

The rowboat shot away from the dock and toward the sea. Emerson released the oars and held on to the sides of the boat, hunkering low. The mermaids had no problem bearing the small vessel at a ridiculous speed.

It was much faster than they'd moved the fishing boat, and even faster than when they'd pushed his homemade raft between Azul and Miren. This time, they knew if they were even a minute too late, another girl would die and become like them.

Emerson looked behind him for a moment and would have laughed out loud had the circumstances been any different. Every person gathered along the fence was staring, mouths hanging open. A lad in a rowboat shooting that fast through the water while the oars lay motionless: nobody knew what to make of it.

He grew more worried as they skirted the coast of the island, heading north.

What would he do when he got there?

He really didn't know. This wasn't something he'd ever planned on, and he had no idea what to expect. All he knew was that if he failed, a girl would die and he would very likely never see his mother again.

Or Saria.

Why does that last thought feel like a knife in my chest?

With shocking clarity, a possible answer to that question pierced the adrenaline coursing through his body. He caught it and tucked it away for later examination. Now was not a good time to be distracted.

SACRIFICE

Emerson hunkered low in the rowboat. The speed at which the mermaids were carrying him along was creating a strong wind. He glanced over the side when he felt a shift in direction. So far, they had been following the coast of Stron Cay, but now the mermaids changed course and angled slightly away from the island.

Does this mean the ritual boat has launched?

Urgency pounded in his ears and he wished they had already arrived at their destination. Would they be too late? Twisting to look behind him, could see the clusters of houses making up the Shaman's village.

There was no fence along the beach.

Only posts in the sand with something tied to them—he couldn't quite make out what—the magical charms that kept the mermaids away, if he had a guess. He clenched his fist as the village rapidly disappeared behind the curve of the watery horizon.

I'm going into this with no plan, he thought. *I really should come up with a plan. Storming the deck of the ship isn't a solo operation. From what Lilyse has told me, the mermaids won't be able to help at all because of the Shaman's magic...*

He sighed in frustration. This was almost certain to be a complete failure. He looked back at the way they'd come, hoping against hope that he would see Mr. Beggley's boat or the governor's.

But he was far, far ahead of them thanks to the mermaids' speed.

He was on his own.

Was it worth it? To probably lose everything for an impossible fool's errand? Was the slightest possibility of saving a life worth losing his?

His chest began to ache and he flinched away from the thoughts of aloneness and how impossible his task was.

All I can do is try. All I can do is try.

Swinging forward, he saw they were rapidly gaining on a boat. It was ornate, painted red with golden scrollwork and a golden figurehead of what he assumed was supposed to be the god of the sea. The mermaids slowed their pace and circled around to the north, positioning him as close to the bow of the boat as they could.

They stopped, unable to go any closer. *The Shaman's magic. It is keeping them away so they can't rescue the sacrifice.* His scalp prickled.

Emerson was surprised no one had spotted his rowboat yet. He looked up at the deck. Every man on the boat was clustered at the starboard rail. Above them, a dozen razor-sharp spear blades flashed in the sun, blinding him. Every man on board was armed. He caught a flash of white between the men crowded at the rail. *White like the dresses the mermaids wear.*

In the center of the group was a tall, dark figure wearing a red cloak. The hood was thrown back to reveal his intricately braided hair. Fiery red. His long beard moved as he spoke.

Emerson strained to hear. The man's voice rose and fell in a husky cadence. A sing-songy rhythm. There was something unnatural and unholy about it. Emerson shivered.

Heart hammering in his chest, and expecting to be discovered any minute, Emerson took up the oars that had laid at rest the whole way so far. The mermaids couldn't help; it was up to him now.

Dipping and pulling the oars, he quietly moved the rowboat closer to the Shaman's vessel. It was agonizingly slow compared to the speed at which he had been traveling.

There was a loud BANG! and he froze, oars hanging in midair just above the water. He was close enough to the ship that the angle was all wrong for seeing the men aboard. But he guessed they had simultaneously slammed the butts of their spears into the deck. The Shaman's voice rose.

"And blessed Sea, receive from our hand this pure sacrifice."

Emerson's heart lurched into his throat. *That's what Lilyse remembers him saying right before—*

There was a scuffle above and something white arched out over the water.

Caramel curls fanned against the blue sky.

Emerson lurched forward in the rowboat as Saria's wild eyes met his just before she disappeared into the seething water.

RESCUE

Emerson's throat was raw and his ears were ringing. Someone was screaming "Noooooo!!!"

It was him.

Not stopping to think, he grabbed at the coiled string of fishing net floats at the bottom of his rowboat and plunged over the side. Letting the floats play out behind him, he kicked and thrashed awkwardly in the water.

Hang it all! He wasn't a great swimmer.

He ducked underneath and opened his eyes. Saria thrashed a few yards away in a swirling cloud of white dress and caramel hair, her hands tied behind her.

Looking all too much like a mermaid. But still solid and very much alive. For now.

She was sinking.

Why is she sinking?!

The men in the boat above had likely tied her to something heavy. Emerson cursed his inability to swim any faster. He kicked himself further down into the deep water, clinging desperately to the end of the floats' rope.

Everything was moving slowly—far, far too slowly. Emerson was jerked short. He looked up.

He had run out of rope.

Saria was just below him. He had to go deeper, but—he had very little confidence in his swimming abilities. And the water was deep, so deep.

She looked up at him, terror filling her beautiful face.

He let go of the rope.

Above, a huge shadow loomed close. It was the ship. The Shaman was hoping to run him down. With two valiant kicks, he reached Saria. Spinning her in the water, he groped at the ropes binding the weight to her wrists.

His lungs were beginning to burn as were his eyes. White dress, ropes, fingers, weight, seaweed. Sinking. It was all a jumble and he couldn't budge the knots.

He gripped her under the arms and kicked desperately, trying to pull her up to the surface with him despite the weight tied to her wrists.

The mermaids could do it despite the heavy weight. Think, Emerson! THINK!

Seaweed.

His mind darted fuzzily to the entry in his mother's book. The Shaman's religion used seaweed for magic.

Through the haze overtaking his brain, he grasped at the seaweed he'd seen attached to the ropes around Saria's wrists. It was wrapped into an intricate, circular charm.

Gripping it with all the strength he had left, he tore it into shreds.

Vaguely, he felt a shift—almost a ripple in the water.

His arms encircling Saria's still form.

Water rushing past him.

Then blinding sunlight. He took a painful, gasping breath. He was lying on his back on top of the waves. Something was supporting him from below the water, and Saria was clutched against his chest.

Was she—?

He squeezed her tighter. She spasmed and coughed seawater. After a moment, her warm breath tickled his neck and she whispered, "Emrie."

He let out a grateful breath.

Something dark bumped against his right arm, and he jumped. It was the rowboat. Somehow he lifted Saria and then himself into it. Peering back over the edge, he could just make out a transparent ripple as one of the mermaids—he wasn't sure which—darted away.

Saria lay curled in a weak ball in the bottom of the rowboat. Emerson worked at the ropes around her wrists, this time successfully getting them off.

"YOU!" a voice roared, causing him to jump. "You have stolen the sacrifice!"

The ritual boat swung toward the small rowboat. His men swarmed over the rigging and the vessel picked up speed.

Shaman Orith stood just behind the figurehead, his eyes burning into Emerson with fury.

"Wrong!" Emerson returned, scrambling to the oars. He would not let this vile man get his hands on Saria again. "You have stolen an innocent girl from her father. And you've done it many times before. You've murdered just to keep your followers more completely under your thumb."

His voice tore harshly across the water as he pulled at the oars. His arms were burning and he was still short of breath. His heart hammered painfully.

The Shaman's face twisted in rage and his red cloak snapped angrily in the stiff breeze propelling his ship.

"You will be dead in a moment, lad," he mocked, "do you really want such foolery to be your last words?"

Emerson sat up straighter. "I do," he said. "Because it isn't foolery if it's the truth."

The chances of them outrunning a wind-powered ship in a boat rowed by a lad who was half-dead a moment ago were slim to none. Emerson knew that. But he could only try.

"Emerson, look!" Saria gasped. She had pulled herself up to a half-sitting position and was staring at something. The water on the port side of Shaman Orith's ship had suddenly begun to writhe.

With a great crack, the ship bucked violently to the left as something impacted it from just under the water. Several men were tossed from the rigging, screaming until they splashed into the water.

PRISONERS

The Shaman clung like a stubborn leaf to the ship's figurehead.

The ship pitched to the other side. Then back again. More and more men were thrown into the water as the ship tossed and bucked as if in a storm of epic proportions.

The mermaids were battering the ship with all the pent-up fury of the last 30 years.

Finally, the Shaman lost his grip on the figurehead and fell to the water below in a shimmering ripple of red. Instantly, the attacks on the ship stopped and it rocked gently in the water as it regained its balance.

A second later, screams punctuated the sudden silence. Saria, looking terrified, reached for Emerson. What new horror was unfolding?

The horror wasn't for them, but for the men in the water as invisible mermaids caught and held them fast.

"They're not going to drown them, are they?" Saria gasped.

Emerson tightened his grip about her. "No, there'd be no justice in that."

"It would be poetic vengeance, perhaps," Saria murmured. Emerson realized she was feeling a strangely close kinship with the mermaids since she had so nearly—no. He couldn't think of that right now. His heart began to hammer again at the very thought of what had almost happened.

And how powerless he had felt.

I'm so glad I knew about their using seaweed to make magical charms. So glad I read that in Mum's book.

He shuddered.

Saria seemed to think he was cold, for she wrapped her arms around his shoulders. He glanced down at her with a grateful smile. He may not be shivering from cold, but the panic that was threatening to blossom in his chest calmed a bit at her embrace. He was grateful.

Someone was cursing wildly and thrashing in the water. Emerson looked up and found that Shaman Orith was floating on his back and being towed toward their rowboat by the unseen hand of a mermaid. The man's blood-red cloak rippled out behind him like a ghastly train.

Emerson clenched his fists both in anger at the sight of the vile man and to stop their nervous shaking.

"Emerson Kadwell! My men told me all about you and your witchcraft! Your meddling! Your foolery!" the man bellowed. He struggled, trying to free his hands from something binding them under the surface of the water.

Emerson blinked. How did this monster not realize everything he had just said about Emerson could easily—and more rightfully—be turned back on him?

"Witchcraft," Saria snorted, trembling, whether from anger or fear Emerson didn't know. Her next words told him. "You're the only one using the stuff around here. But a man with a brain to solve problems and a heart that propels him to do so—he destroyed your magic! And, as your spies probably told you already, everyone now knows what you've been doing and why. The mermaids are finally getting justice," she finished indignantly.

Emerson wondered why the mermaid had dragged the Shaman over to them in the first place. He peered into the water, shading his eyes from the bright sunshine. In the shadow made by the Shaman and his large cloak, he could just make out the face of Danae.

He smiled. *She's been waiting a long, long time for this moment.*

She beamed up at him and nodded her head in thanks. She seemed to understand he didn't have his speaking tube with him and that he certainly didn't want to put his head under the water again anytime soon.

He felt his throat swell and a wetness form in the corners of his eyes. He gave her a solemn nod. She then pointed south, and he looked up.

Something was coming over the horizon. No, two—three. They were boats.

"Who is that?" Saria asked, her eyebrows pinching together in worry.

"I think it's your father."

"Oh—!" she hiccuped, looking watery-eyed and relieved.

Emerson squinted at the other ships. "And if I had my guess, Governor Milus and his deputies as well."

Danae towed a still-cursing Shaman Orith away. She joined the other mermaids holding their captives in a cluster near the emptied ritual boat.

Emerson turned and found Saria hunkered down in the bottom of the rowboat.

"What's the matter?" he asked, instantly worried.

"Um—" she said uncomfortably. "I just realized I'm rather soaked through, and there are others coming—"

"Right!" Emerson said, suddenly equally uncomfortable. He didn't recall anything about her appearance seeming untoward, but he nevertheless rummaged through the random items in the bottom of the rowboat and passed her an empty gunny sack he found. All without looking her way.

"Thank you, Emerson," she said with a grateful sigh. "This will do." He turned and smiled at her. She had draped the gunny sack around the shoulders of her sopping dress like a towel.

"For whatever it's worth you seemed fine to me, never better, actually—err... never mind." He bit his lip and glanced away. That hadn't come out right at all.

When he turned, she was a pretty shade of pink and was trying to avoid eye contact. But a tiny smile played around her lips, so Emerson knew he hadn't ruined anything.

After several minutes, Mr. Beggley's boat was anchored alongside the rowboat, and they were being helped up a rope ladder. Once on the deck of the larger vessel, someone handed both of them proper towels.

Saria was crushed in her father's embrace. Emerson thought he saw both of them crying so he turned away to give them privacy. Madge reached her arms out to him. In lieu of his mother being there, Lilyse's mother and the mother-figure to his best friend would certainly do.

He gave her a wet and shaky hug. "Thank you ever so much for everything, Emerson Kadwell," she whispered. "You gave me another chance for a goodbye with my daughter and saved the girl who's become like a daughter to me these many years. You're a strong lad and a good one."

Emerson didn't think anyone had ever called him strong before. *There must be more than one kind of strength,* he decided, swallowing back the lump in his throat.

Madge released him and Mr. Beggley fervently shook his hand and then, deeming that insufficient, he pulled him in for a hug and a quick clap on the shoulder. "I can't thank you enough, lad. I never can. What that vile man tried to do…"

Remembering Shaman Orith and his men were being held prisoner by the mermaids, they made their way to the stern of Mr. Beggley's boat.

"Would you look at that," Mr. Beggley said under his breath.

The men were being transferred to the deputies' boat under the watchful eye of Governer Milus from his own vessel. The mermaids had already tied their hands behind their backs with…

"Seaweed," Emerson snorted, exchanging satisfied glances with Saria.

GOODBYES

It was evening when *The Daphne* approached the Chadwick docks. Emerson went to the bow of the boat and leaned forward. Something was different.

He stared for a while before he realized what it was.

The fence was gone. The beach sloped, uninterrupted, from the water, and several figures with torches hurried down to the docks.

A tingle ran up his spine. His village was no longer living in fear of the mermaids. They had embraced the truth and had no need for fences.

Two figures were waiting on the dock, the tall, burly one holding a torch high. The smaller one was instantly recognizable to Emerson.

"Mum!" he shouted, waving.

The boat dropped anchor and Emerson was the first to disembark. His mother hurried to him, wrapping him in a tight embrace. He bent and returned her hug.

She let go and held him at arm's length. Her eyes were gleaming in the torchlight. "I'm so proud of you, Emrie."

He smiled. "But you don't even know how it went! I haven't yet said whether we succeeded."

She smiled knowingly. "I can tell from your face that you did. And even if it hadn't been a success, I would still be proud of you. You've grown into a good, good man."

Swallowing the lump in his throat and the words that refused to come out, Emerson gave her another tight hug.

Cyrus approached, torch in one hand. For once the big man didn't say anything. The corners of his mouth turned up slightly. He gave Emerson a nod and a quick clap on the shoulder.

Emerson waited in silence. The moon sailed high above him, lighting the Chadwick shore with soft, clear light. The waves dashed past his bare feet and up beyond the place where he sat, soaking the seat of his trousers.

He didn't care. He was getting used to the water.

The weather was becoming more stable, more inclined to warmth in the two days since he had returned home. Summer was fast approaching.

The gentle swish of the water rolling past him nearly lulled him to sleep, but he shook himself and stared harder into the waves. He had known that Madge was spending most of her evenings down by the water, visiting with Lilyse. Making up for the time that had been lost and preparing for the final goodbye.

Any day now, the Shaman's trial on Stron Cay would conclude. He hadn't wanted to intrude on their limited time, so he had kept away from the beach in the evenings. Tonight, however Madge had come by the cottage and insisted he take a turn. She said Lilyse wanted to speak to him.

He folded his hands over his knees and hummed softly, lost in thought about everything that had occurred. Moments later, Lilyse appeared before him in the water. She was biting her lip and tears streamed down her cheeks.

Emerson furrowed his brows. "Hello," he said into the speaking tube. "What is it?"

Swallowing hard, Lilyse extended her hand. Emerson reach forward into the water and took it. "Nothing," she said. "You were just humming my sea shanty is all."

Emerson hadn't realized it. Now, it was his turn to swallow hard. It felt like there was a rock in his throat, and his eyes stung with unshed tears.

"I am going to miss you, Lilyse. Even when I didn't know it, you've always been here for me. You're leaving me with a great gift. I now know that I have what it takes to do the right thing no matter what it costs me. I have that kind of strength. Strange as it may seem... you've taught me how to hear others."

She quirked an eyebrow.

"Yes," he admitted, feeling his face heat, "I'm talking about Saria. She's not such an annoying girl after all, you know?"

Lilyse laughed musically through her tears. "No, she is not at all. I'm so very happy you will still have her as your friend when I'm gone. And, Emerson?"

"Hmm?"

"Don't miss it."

"Don't miss what?"

She shook her head, regarding him bemusedly. "You'll know."

Her face grew serious.

This was goodbye. He could feel it.

"Emerson, I want you to know something. Ever since you were the little tyke who got lost in the waves, you've been saving me."

"I saved... you?" he asked, bewildered.

"Yes," she said, her sweet voice muffled, as usual, by the sound of the water all around them. How he wished he could hear her clearly for once. "For the first three years after my death, I had been wandering the sea, lost and angry and oh, so bitter. The bitterness was eating me and it was worse than death, even worse than being trapped between life and death.

"But when I came upon you, struggling in the waves, helpless and alone, I couldn't help but comfort you and swim you back to shore. It was the first thing

I had done for someone else since the day of my sacrifice. Saving you saved me. And now, any day now, you will have saved me again.

"Emerson Kadwell," she took both of his hands and gazed at him with an ocean of feeling, "I will be eternally grateful."

Emerson found he was completely devoid of words. He held her hands tightly, mutely.

This will be our last time meeting. How can I have no words?!

"Sometimes silence is a good thing. A healing thing, Emerson," she said as if reading his thoughts. They sat quietly for several minutes, the waves dancing up and down the beach being the only sound.

He made no effort to conceal the tears. He didn't pull his hands away to brush the wetness from his face. Right then, it didn't matter whether the strongest of sailors would be crying unashamedly in the same situation.

What mattered was that Lilyse was going away and he would miss her.

BEGINNINGS

The next evening, Emerson went by the Beggleys' house after supper and asked Saria if she would like to walk down to the shore with him. She agreed, and in a short time, they sat side by side at the top of the cliff.

He wanted to watch for the mermaids. It seemed fitting that Saria be there too.

Emerson removed his cap and rested it on his knees. A perfect breeze, not too warm and not too cold, played through his wild, dark hair.

The bright rays of sun had just disappeared beyond the horizon, dousing the golden water in greyness.

His mind replayed the events of the past weeks as it had almost every day since returning to the island of Azul. It was still remarkable to him that he and Saria were alive, even more so in some ways that he had finally been believed.

The light continued to fail as they sat in companionable silence. Emerson leaned forward, straining to see a blueish glow in the waves that would tell him Lilyse, Danae, Susette, or any of the others were near.

The grey waters were barren. Sometime in the past day, the courts on Stron Cay must have completed their work.

Saria laid a hand on his arm. They stared out to sea for a while longer, the breeze and the sound of the waves lulling them until time seemed to stand still even as it passed.

"They're gone," Saria whispered.

Emerson nodded silently, feeling a sudden stab of loneliness. The seas were empty. The mermaids rested. This was bittersweet beyond what he could have imagined.

"You did it," Saria said. Her voice contained a smile, but quavered just slightly. "You really, did it, Emrie." She squeezed his arm and then rested her head against his shoulder.

"Yes, I suppose I did." He looked down at her. "Really, though *we* did."

She looked up to meet his gaze. "What will you do next?"

A smile played around Emerson's lips. "Several people in the village have asked me to work on inventions they would find useful. Other than that— whatever is right." He looked back out toward the water and fell into a deep reverie.

What could have been minutes or hours later, Emerson gradually became aware of Saria's voice.

"—lost in your thoughts. I could tease you to get your attention, I suppose. But I'm all grown up now, so... I won't. I do have a new idea about how to get you to pay attention, though—"

Emerson suddenly snapped fully out of his thoughts. Saria had pressed a quick, but deliciously warm kiss to his cheek. He whipped his head sideways to look at her.

She was smiling up at him. "Well, that worked!" she said quietly.

Emerson felt heat rise up his neck. "Sorry, were you talking? Was—was I not...?"

"No, you weren't," she said, peacefully leaning against his shoulder again.

EMERSON AND SARIA RETURN IN···

PHANTOMS

THANK YOU TO···

My incredible Wattpad readers. Your constant cheering for this novel really kept me going. I *knew* I had a good story thanks to your enjoyment of it. ALL the hugs to you!

My man and most favorite person. You made time for me to write and let me read it to you even though you thought *maybe* it was kind of a girl story. And then you ended up loving it. That means the world to me!

My sister for assuring me the story wasn't awful, meaningless fluff.

Everyone who helped in any little way: from voting on your favorite cover design, to sharing about it with friends and family. You are just the best!

ABOUT DENVER

Denver is a fun-sized person who dislikes talking about herself in third person. (Feels pretentious, ya know?) She lives with her handsome hubby and an army of small gnomes that look suspiciously like the two of them combined. She spends her days desperate to write a good story without too many dumb typos.

She thrives on hearing from her fans. (Like, really!)

Connect with her online: denverevans.wordpress.com

Facebook: hyperurl.co/denverfb

Instagram: @denverevansauthor